MISSING

A Perfect Vacation.
A Perfect Nightmare.

A THRILLER BY
CHRISTY COOPER-BURNETT

Black Rose Writing | Texas

ISBN: 978-1-68513-519-5
PUBLISHED BY BLACK ROSE WRITING
www.blackrosewriting.com

Printed in the United States of America
Suggested Retail Price (SRP) $19.95

Missing is printed in Calluna

*As a planet-friendly publisher, Black Rose Writing does its best to eliminate unnecessary waste to reduce paper usage and energy costs, while never compromising the reading experience. As a result, the final word count vs. page count may not meet common expectations.

PRAISE FOR
MISSING

"Mother and daughter are forced to break all the rules to survive in this fast-paced thriller filled with betrayal and redemption."
–Gary Gerlacher, author of *The Last Patient of the Night*

"You'll think twice about booking your next getaway after reading this tale of a perfect vacation gone horribly wrong."
–Regina Buttner, author of *The Revenge Paradox*

"Cooper-Burnett weaves together a narrative filled with riveting action sequences and adrenaline-fueled confrontations. *Missing* brings to light a harrowing issue while celebrating the indomitable spirit of the will to survive."
–Ellen Ricciutti, author of *One Time or Another*

For my son, Mychael

MISSING

PROLOGUE

I wish I could say I never saw this coming. That even in my wildest dreams, I never imagined ending up here. That it had been a complete shock, and therefore there was nothing I could have done to prevent it. But that would be a lie. The truth was my fear of something like this happening almost prevented me from boarding the ship. From the very beginning, I was terrified to embark on this cruise, constantly worried about all the things that could go wrong. I wouldn't be surprised if I actually manifested this into reality with my persistent anxiety. Even now, as I raced through the labyrinth of narrow passageways beneath the main deck of the *Jewel of the Sea*, I couldn't escape the truth. Something bad *had* happened, leaving me trapped in a desperate situation with no obvious way out.

My bare feet slapped loudly against the shiny floor, echoing through the cramped space. I cast a furtive glance over my shoulder. No one was chasing me. Yet.

I knew it was only a matter of time before he came after me. Hopelessly lost, I forced myself to keep moving, despite the burning sensation in my lungs and the cramp in my leg, trying to get to one of the upper passenger decks where I could find help. Not knowing where I was, I knew I had to keep moving because every second counted in this cat-and-mouse game.

The area below the passenger decks was an entirely different world. Unlike the festive, bright colors adorning every available space of the rest of the ship, below deck, I was engulfed in a bleak world of gray and dimness. My only thought at that moment was to get away. But my head was fuzzy and I felt confused. Whatever drugs my captors spiked my water with had left me feeling disoriented. I couldn't believe my own stupidity for not expecting them to drug me. When they took me, I resisted, so it should have been no surprise that they would try to keep me quiet after capturing me. However, my fear and dehydration at the time clouded my thinking. Plus, my thoughts were going wild as I tried to make sense of why this was happening to me.

Running blindly through the hallway with no real plan, I narrowly avoided colliding with someone as I barreled around a corner. Seeing his white shirt and black shoulder epaulets confirmed he was a crew member of the *Jewel of the Sea*, and instant relief flooded through me.

"Help me!" I sobbed, my eyes brimming with fresh tears. "There's a man and he's going to come after me. He had me tied up in a room. He's trying to kidnap me!"

"Whoa, calm down, miss," replied the crew member, gripping my shoulders while he tried to steady me. I shook my head in response.

"No! I need you to call security, please! He could find me any minute!"

"Okay, I understand. Just give me a minute. I'm calling right now. See?" He unclipped the handheld radio from his belt and held it up for me to see, then took a few steps away and spoke quietly into his radio. My eyes darted around the hall, scanning every corner, as I continued to search for someone chasing me. I pressed my back against the wall and sank into a crouching position, relieved when there was no sign of anyone. My thoughts then turned to my mom, who had come on this cruise with me and who I knew must be worried sick about me. I needed to find her and let her know I was safe.

The crew member finished his conversation and took a step toward me, extending his hand to help me up. "I've alerted the head of security and he will meet us on an upper deck. It's just a short walk. Can you make it?" he asked.

"Yes," I said, grabbing his hand and straightening up.

He guided me through the maze of hallways where a sign caught my attention, identifying the space as level E-3. The service level. I must have been held on this level the entire time, because I hadn't been moved up or down. How did my kidnapper keep me concealed on the service level? There would be constant foot traffic with staff in and out.

Wouldn't there?

While I was trying to solve this, we turned a corner, and I froze in my tracks. The man who had taken me by force, the same man I was frightened would find me again, leaned casually against the wall, one foot propped up for support. He glanced up from his phone and flashed me a grin, as if we were old friends. Pushing himself off the wall, he made his way toward us. My heart hammered wildly in my chest as my mind struggled to catch up.

"Megan. There you are. I was afraid I'd lost you. Thank you, Mateo. I'll take it from here," he said, inching nearer.

I turned to flee, but Mateo intercepted me by grabbing my arm and forcefully pinning me against the wall. My kidnapper closed the gap between us, still grinning. I watched the smile slide from his face, replaced with a cold stare. He twisted my hands behind my back, securing them with a zip tie.

"No," I cried, knowing it wouldn't change anything.

"Come on, Megan. Don't fight it. Your buyer will be ready to pick you up tomorrow night, and I expect you to be compliant and in good shape by then."

With his fingers digging painfully into the flesh of my upper arm, he pulled me forward as any remaining hope I had diminished. I knew right then that I wouldn't make it out, and something cold slid through me at the thought of it. I had botched my one shot at getting away.

I was on the brink of being sold to the highest bidder, thrust into a harsh reality I couldn't make sense of. It was my worst nightmare come true.

CHAPTER ONE

Megan
THREE WEEKS EARLIER

"This isn't working. I wanna break up."

I couldn't wrap my head around what I was hearing. I blinked at Brian once and opened my mouth to say something, but he raised his hands to quiet me.

"I know you probably think this is coming out of nowhere, but it's not. I've been struggling with this for a while now. God, Megan, we don't do anything anymore. You won't go anywhere. We never do anything fun together!"

Was he for real? No. He couldn't be serious. The venue was booked. Invitations were printed. *I bought my freaking wedding dress.* This had to be a bad prank. Maybe he was having a stroke. Or maybe he had a brain tumor. Because truthfully, that would be the only way to explain the bombshell he had just dumped in my lap.

"This isn't funny, Brian."

"You're right. It isn't funny at all. Look, I don't want to hurt your feelings, Megan, but I just can't do this anymore," he said, collapsing into the overstuffed chair in the corner of our living room. "We don't want the same things out of life. We just don't fit together like we used to. I'm not happy."

He didn't want to hurt my feelings? Oh, puh-leeze. He was dumping me. What did he think that was going to do, boost my self-esteem?

"Where is this coming from, Brian? You knew the type of person I was when we met three years ago. I haven't changed. *You* have! And I don't understand why any of this is an issue all of a sudden. We're in the middle of planning our wedding! Your timing for a premature midlife crisis really sucks rocks."

He ran his hands through his hair, a gesture I used to find adorable, but at that moment, it just screamed impatience.

"I know my timing isn't great. I get it," he replied, rising to his feet again and wandering around the room, releasing a heavy sigh. "You're boring. There, I said it," he declared, raising and dropping his arms dramatically. "I don't know how else to put it, honestly. And I'm sorry, but you need to hear it. You're more fearful than ever, Megan. You're scared of absolutely everything!"

"Don't be ridiculous. I'm not scared of *everything*. And I'm not boring, I'm careful. There's a difference. And not only is your timing for a meltdown *not great*, as you put it, but I can't think of a worse time for it. Whatever this is, Brian, you need to snap out of it, because we're walking down the aisle in three months."

He lowered his eyes for a minute before delivering his next blow. "I met someone else."

The beating of my pulse filled my ears, and I was certain I didn't hear him correctly. "What?" It was the only thing I could manage to squeak out.

"I met someone, Megs."

Megs? Really? I bristled at the use of his nickname for me. This was most definitely not a cutesy nickname kind of conversation. I mean, seriously, read the room, Brian.

"*Excuse me?* What do you mean, you met someone else?" I said, a chuckle escaping me, although there was nothing funny about what he'd just said. "Who? Where? *When?*"

"Her name is Leticia. She's my skydiving instructor. She's fun, Megan. She's bold and adventurous, and she's not afraid of life the way you are. This breakup will be the best thing for both of us. I know it may not seem like that now, but trust me, over time, you'll see I'm right."

"No. No, no, no! You have got to be joking." I sprang up from the couch and began pacing, my hands gesturing wildly as I talked. "You're leaving me for your skydiving instructor? Ninety days away from our wedding? You cannot be serious! What will our parents think? And our friends? Have you lost your mind, Brian? Wait, I know what this is. You have cold feet, that's all. It's normal. So you've had your little *fling*, and now you can end it. I mean, obviously, it will take some time and effort for me to even *begin* to forgive this betrayal, because I am so angry with you right now I could scream! But breaking up and canceling our wedding? No. Not happening."

Faced with his silence, I turned to confront him. "How could you do this to me, Brian?" I cried.

He looked away without responding, and I took a moment to take a couple of deep breaths and compose myself. "Okay. Let's calm down. With some work, obviously some couples counseling, we can get past this," I said.

He shook his head. "No, Megan. This isn't cold feet. I don't feel the same way about you anymore. I'm in love with Leticia. I didn't plan it. It just happened. We're going to Mexico to her cousin's place and getting married there next month. I'm sorry. But I've made my choice. I choose her."

I guess that was supposed to make me feel better. Knowing that he didn't plan to cheat on me and leave me in the middle of planning our wedding. It took a second for the rest of his words to register with me. He was in love with her? He chose her? That was absurd. This wasn't *The Bachelor*. This was our life. He proposed to me, not her.

He loved *me*. He *loves* me.

At least up until five minutes ago, I was sure he did. I just needed to remind him of that. And pray for a miracle. I sank down on the couch, my legs suddenly shaky. The new couch we bought together just a month ago. I admit I hadn't exactly been girlfriend of the year material. But I was *not* boring. Okay, I was super cautious. Some people might even say I was fearful. I would give him that much. But just because I didn't like to skydive or zipline or white-water raft or any of the other über-dangerous activities Brian liked to do didn't mean I was boring. *Did it?*

"I'm going to go pack a few things. I'll get my other stuff later in the week. You can keep all the furniture and everything. I don't want to disrupt your life any further."

He didn't want to disrupt my life any further. How exceedingly thoughtful of him. The cheating jerk. At least we kept our bank accounts separate, not planning to combine them until after the wedding. Of course, that simply made it easier for Brian to pull up stakes and move on now. How fortunate for him.

Brian started down the hall for our bedroom, but I was glued to the couch. For a split second, I considered following him and begging him to stay. But what was the point? If he didn't want to continue our relationship, I couldn't force him to. Tears spilled from my eyes and ran down my cheeks. I wiped them away hastily, angry at myself for crying. I didn't want to be emotional. I wanted to give my anger my full focus.

Twenty minutes later, my now ex-fiancé emerged from our shared bedroom with two suitcases, presumably ready to head off to his new bedroom. At the house he would share with his bold, adventurous skydiving instructor, Leticia. *Barf.*

I couldn't even look at him. I was so hurt. And angry. It hadn't taken me long to morph from disbelief and broken-heartedness into majorly pissed off at him. He'd slink off into the sunset scot-free and leave me to deal with canceling the wedding, calling vendors, and revoking invitations. The very thought of it was so degrading. What a nightmare.

He'd jet off to his destination wedding in Mexico next month without a care in the world, while I was stuck here to clean up the mess. It wasn't fair. Why should he be allowed to walk away from this unscathed?

"So, I'll be in touch to work out the financial stuff and pick up my other things. I don't plan on leaving you to shoulder all the expenses. I'll be as fair as possible. I'm truly sorry, Megs. I never wanted to hurt you."

"Yeah. You said that already," I responded, thinking I did a fairly decent job of not sounding too bitter. I honestly wanted to slap him, but I knew that would be going a step too far. Instead, I glared at him long enough to make him uncomfortable enough to leave.

I don't know how long I remained on the couch feeling sorry for myself, but eventually, I got up and poured myself a glass of wine, grabbed a bag of Doritos and a pint of Ben & Jerry's Chunky Monkey ice cream. Admittedly, not my best move, as I was clearly eating my feelings. I would normally never indulge in those kind of snacks. Brian always bought junk food, while I had always been so cautious about what I ate and I maintained a balanced, healthy diet.

And there was that word again. *Cautious.* Was that really such a bad personality trait to have? I didn't think so.

I wallowed in self-pity for the rest of the evening, flipping through mindless TV programs and stuffing chips in my face between spoonfuls of ice cream and sips of wine. I landed on a reality show about cheating spouses caught in the act, which only fueled my anger at Brian. I finally forced myself to go to bed at eleven o'clock, but not before changing the sheets, because I couldn't bear to sleep on them when Brian had slept there just the night before. I slipped into our king-size bed and hugged his pillow to my chest tightly.

Then I cried myself to sleep. It appeared that my meticulously constructed and overly cautious life was slowly unraveling.

CHAPTER TWO

Megan

As the sun rose, I reluctantly dragged myself out of bed just before my six o'clock alarm the following morning. I woke up at stupid o'clock the night before and only dozed off again right before I had to get up for the day. So not only was I hungover, but I was exhausted too. A perfect combination.

My head screamed for painkillers, so I rummaged through my bedside drawer for two Tylenol and washed them down with a gulp of water from the bottle on my nightstand before I even swung my feet over the side of the bed.

My mind went back to the previous night's events, and I remembered Brian was gone. For a minute, I thought I might be sick. I rushed to the bathroom and steadied myself over the sink while I dragged in deep breaths of air. Despite my better judgment, I looked at my reflection before I stepped into the shower. That was a mistake. Crying had left my eyes red and puffy, and my hair was a complete disaster. It resembled a rat's nest.

My gaze was drawn to the wine stain on my pajama shirt. I was a total wreck, and I seriously considered calling in sick to work. Then I envisioned myself spending the entire day at home alone, rambling around the empty house, reminders of Brian everywhere, and I realized that would be even worse than managing my classroom of five-year-olds.

Taking a hot shower marginally enhanced my physical state. Mentally, however, I was all over the map. I was angry at Brian. Then I missed him. The thought of him with someone else made me cry again. That was how it continued while I got ready for work. Cycling through the different stages of grief and anger over and over again. I skipped my usual mascara altogether. Considering I knew I would cry later, it would be a waste of time and have me looking like a depressed racoon by the end of the day.

I made myself a cup of coffee and a slice of toast, just to have something in my stomach, even though I had no appetite. Drinking black coffee on an empty stomach was sure to give me a stomachache, and adding that to my list of ailments was the last thing I needed. I had enough going on between my headache and sleep exhaustion.

After I finished my breakfast, I pushed myself off the barstool at my kitchen counter, grabbed my tote bag and lunch, and headed for the door. The sun assaulted me immediately, the brightness forcing my eyes shut like a vampire. I squinted and found my way to the car, where I immediately fished out my sunglasses.

I was grateful that the ride to work was quick and uneventful, and I used the time to gather my thoughts. Meaning I tried to tamp down my anger at Brian so it didn't eat away at me all day. It was no surprise that it didn't work, and by the time I pulled into the parking lot, I was near tears again. I took a couple of deep breaths and steeled myself for the onslaught of kindergarteners I was about to face.

My classroom, with its colorful construction paper art projects and finger paintings covering the walls, was a stark contrast to my mood. My students wouldn't arrive for another thirty minutes, so I focused on getting organized while I tried to think of anything but Brian. I skipped putting my lunch in the teacher's lounge refrigerator so I didn't have to see any of my coworkers, but I should have known that my best friend, Tracy, would come looking for me.

And she did. My classroom door opened and Tracy breezed in to plant herself on the corner of my desk.

"What's up, buttercup?"

I looked up at her, wondering if I could get away with postponing telling her. I really didn't want to say it out loud. I hadn't told anyone about Brian yet because then there would be no going back. It would be real. And I didn't want to face reality yet, some part of me secretly hoping there was still some way to fix things with him. Although deep down I knew that wasn't possible, and I couldn't stop the tears that slid down my cheeks.

"Hey, what's wrong?" she said, rushing to my side.

"Brian left me. He broke up with me. He's marrying someone else next month," I said, the words rushing out of me before I could stop them.

Tracy pulled back and stared at me in disbelief. "What? Brian left you? But you're getting married in a few months."

"Was. I *was* getting married in a few months. Now he's going to marry his skydiving instructor in Mexico next month. *Leticia*," I said, unable to keep the venom from my voice when I said her name.

"Oh, honey," she said, kneeling in front of me and taking my hands in hers. "Mexico? With his skydiving instructor? Seriously? That idiot. What is he thinking? Well, evidently, he's not thinking. He'll come to his senses; you'll see."

I shook my head. "No. As much as I'd like to believe that, truthfully, I could never trust him after this. Never," I said.

"That's understandable. But you're going to be fine. You're a badass. You don't need a douche bag like Brian to be happy. I hope *Banditos* storm his wedding."

I laughed because no one who knew me would ever describe me as being a badass. The tears continued to roll down my face, and I gave myself a mental pat on the back for my decision not to wear mascara. Although I hadn't thought the crying would start this early.

I wiped my eyes as the first bell rang. Tracy gave me a look wrought with pity, and I got a glimpse of what I was sure would be one of many sympathetic looks to come. I wanted to go home, crawl back into bed, and hide under the blankets. Instead, I allowed my pity party to continue in full swing for the rest of the day.

The highlight of my afternoon was when Cynthia Taylor poured glue all over Caleb Murphy's art project when he called her ugly. At least Cynthia stood up for herself and was preparing for the real world where boys called you mean names. Like ugly and boring. I silently cheered her on, thinking one point for us girls.

School went okay for the rest of the day. I worked through lunch to avoid having to socialize. I supervised finger painting. We practiced our ABCs. I read the class a story. The kids were oblivious to my broken heart. Which was great because I was kind of a mess emotionally. A group of high schoolers would have picked up on my mental headspace immediately and made my life miserable all day. But I was teaching kindergartners. Thank goodness for small miracles.

At the end of the workday, I hurried to my car, not wanting to see any of the other teachers and become caught up in a conversation. I didn't have the energy to pretend everything was all right. Plus, I couldn't trust myself not to bawl like a baby, and frankly, I was sick of crying.

Once inside my car, I stared at my phone for a minute, dreading doing what I knew I must. I was closer to my mom than most daughters were. I told her everything, and she knew where all the bodies were buried, so to speak. I also knew the news about me and Brian would send her spiraling into full-on mother bear capacity. My hangover was still lurking around the fringes of my head, and I really wanted to delay telling her. But I knew if I did, it would simply make things worse. I inhaled a deep breath and hit the speed dial number in the favorites section of my phone.

It only rang once before she picked it up.

"Hi, sweetie! I was just thinking about you. How was your day?"

"Hi, Mom. Um, I'm okay, I guess."

"Uh-oh. Don't try to fool me, Megan. I'm your mother. I can tell when something is wrong. Spill it."

A sob escaped me before I could stop it. "Brian broke up with me." The words tumbled out, and I immediately regretted not rephrasing them to a gentler version of the truth.

I heard my mother gasp through the phone and imagined the look of horror on her face.

"What? That little ass. I'm on my way over."

"No! Mom, please. It's been a long day and I need to sleep. I tossed and turned all night. I'm fine." I was far from fine, but I wanted some time alone to sort out my feelings a bit more.

"Mom?" I said. But I was too late. She had already hung up, and I pictured her sprinting to her car. I pulled the Tylenol from my purse and swallowed two pills. I had a feeling I was going to need them.

CHAPTER THREE

Michelle

I was furious after ending the call with my daughter, Megan. It wasn't a complete shock that Brian had walked out on her. I have to be honest; I was never a fan of his. My daughter is a beautiful, kind, generous, and compassionate woman. It wasn't as if Brian was a terrible person, but they were beyond mismatched.

When Megan was a little girl, she was always different. Most kids ran headfirst into their next adventure. Not my daughter. Even at five years old, she would hesitate before she rode her bike around the track in the open field next to our house. The other children would ride fearlessly, leaping over dirt hills and engaging in races with each other. Megan would cautiously ride her bicycle to the field's edge, then walk it onto the track and slowly navigate around the field. That overly cautious approach to life stuck with her into adulthood, and to say that she was not a fan of anything adventurous was an understatement.

Brian was the complete opposite. He loved skydiving, white-water rafting, bungee jumping, snowboarding, and anything else that gave him an adrenaline rush. Their relationship was destined to fail right from the start. I hated to say I told you so, but I *had* told her so.

Within a minute of our phone call, my brain kicked into overdrive. It was purely natural for me to rush to my daughter's side. I heard her object when I said I was coming over. Don't judge me, but that's why I hung up. She might not think she needed me, but I knew she did, and there was no way I was going to abandon her when her world had just blown up. Would it be another matter if they had just been dating? Probably not, to be honest. I would still rush over there. Ending an engagement was significant, and calling off the wedding wouldn't be easy for Megan. As that thought sank in, I realized I needed backup.

I dialed my best friend, Rochelle, who was like an aunt to Megan. She picked up the phone after the first ring.

"Hey, gorgeous, what's shakin'?"

"The little pissant broke up with Megan. Can you believe it? Well, of course you can. We knew this was coming."

I listened to Rochelle's sharp intake of air on the other end of the phone. "Seriously? But the wedding is only a few months away! Oh my God. This is terrible."

"Can I pick you up on the way over to Megan's?"

"Don't you dare try to go without me. I'll meet you outside in ten," she said, hanging up.

I knew Rochelle would be as enraged over this development as I was. She loved Megan, and like me, she didn't particularly like Brian. We had secretly nicknamed him the pissant.

Snatching my car keys off the hall table, I quickly glanced at my reflection in the mirror hanging above it. I gave my hair a quick fluff and swiped on some lip gloss before stepping out and getting into my car.

I drove through Taco Bell since it was the only fast food Megan would eat. And this was definitely a fast-food kind of night. The girl was too healthy for her own good. I kept telling her to live a little, but it always fell on deaf ears.

When I pulled up in front of Rochelle's house fifteen minutes later, she was sitting on the porch swing on her cell phone. She seemed to be engaged in a serious conversation, and she didn't appear to be pleased about it. After a moment, she ended the call and waved before heading toward my car.

"How is she?" she asked, settling into the passenger seat and buckling her seatbelt as her text alert chimed.

"I'm not sure. I hung up on her before she could say much."

Rochelle lifted her gaze from her phone and looked in my direction. "You did what?"

"I had to, Rochelle. She started to tell me not to come over. It was better that I pretended not to hear her. No way was I going to stay away when she obviously needs me."

"Maybe she really just needs a little space to process things."

It was my turn to look at Rochelle. "What? Since when does Megan know what's best for her? I'm her mother. She may feel numb right now, but this is going to hit her hard, and when it does, she is going to fall apart. You know I'm right, Rochelle."

"I suppose you're right. But just promise me that if she doesn't want us there, we can leave. Okay?" she said, focusing on her phone again.

I let out a chuckle in response to Rochelle's comment. She knew me better than that. I was going to be there for my daughter, no matter what. It's what I did. And there was no way I was going to stop now.

Rochelle seemed distracted as she remained engrossed in texting on her phone.

"What's going on with you? You seem irritated and you haven't put down your phone once since I picked you up," I said, glancing over at her.

"Oh, I just had a small setback with one of my investments. I'm working on a solution."

She shifted in her seat to face me. "I have an idea, Michelle. Why don't we invite Megan on our upcoming cruise?"

"Oh, I don't know, Rochelle. You know how Megan is. I can't imagine her agreeing to go on a cruise. Especially with a couple of old broads like us."

"I know. But it would do her good to get away for a week. Somewhere free from constant reminders of Brian."

"I know you're right. It would be good for her. I'm just not sure she'll agree to it."

"Well, we'll just have to make her see that it's what she needs. You'll think of a way. You always do," she said, tossing her phone into her purse.

As I drove to Megan's, my mind was completely absorbed with the thought of her coming on the cruise with us. Rochelle's point was indeed a good one. A change of scenery would do Megan a world of good, and the idea grew on me the more I thought about it. By the time I pulled into Megan's driveway, I had already made up my mind. She couldn't miss going on the cruise with us. If she didn't agree to go after a few subtle suggestions, I would resort to more forceful measures. I told myself I was only doing it with her best interests in mind. As her mother, I knew what was best for her. While she might not share the same opinion, it was my responsibility to look after her. And I took that responsibility very seriously.

CHAPTER FOUR

Megan

I pulled into my driveway, surprised that my mother's car wasn't already parked there waiting for me to get home. Maybe she had actually listened to me for once in her life and respected my need for space. Right. I had obviously just beat her to my house.

My body was thoroughly drained when I got inside, and all I wanted to do was grab a quick bite to eat and collapse on my bed to watch TV. Despite my lack of energy and the desire not to, I still couldn't stop myself from thinking about my last conversation with Brian. The comment that stung the most was him calling me boring. We had been together for three years, and up until now, he had never complained. Thinking about it some more, I had to admit that wasn't entirely true. He always asked me to join him in extreme sports, but that just wasn't my thing. And he knew that going into a relationship with me.

So what had changed? *Leticia.* That's what changed. She showed up and destroyed everything Brian and I had built over our years together. I couldn't help but wonder if she knew he was engaged. And if that were true, what kind of woman started a relationship with a man who was already engaged? The spoiled, selfish, entitled kind, I told myself.

I undressed and tossed my work clothes in the hamper, then got into pajamas. It was only four in the afternoon, but I didn't care. I slid my feet into slippers and padded down the hall to the kitchen. Opening the refrigerator, I stared at the meager contents before settling on a toasted cheese sandwich and more Ben & Jerry's. I had everything gathered on the counter when the doorbell interrupted me. I sighed and headed to the living room, knowing it was my mother. I also knew she wouldn't go away. But I still looked through the peephole to be sure it was her. I was nothing if not prudent. I rolled my eyes at myself, thinking Brian was right. It was possible that I tended to be overly cautious.

Oh God. She brought reinforcements.

My mother and her best friend, Rochelle, stood on my porch with a bag from Taco Bell, my guilty pleasure. That explained the delay in my mother getting here. Even though I dreaded it with every fiber of my being and knew I would regret it, I opened the door.

My mom was halfway inside before the door was fully opened. "Sweetheart. Are you okay?" she asked, hugging me close. She stepped back, frowning. "What are you wearing?"

I thought the sheep patterned flannels gave it away, but I answered anyway. "Hi, Mom. I'm wearing pajamas."

"It's not even five o'clock yet. You poor darling. I brought your favorite fast food. Get inside before the neighbors see you this way and think you never got dressed this morning. You *did* get dressed today, didn't you?"

"Yes, Mother. Of course I got dressed today. I just got home from work."

She pulled me into another hug, and I grimaced and rolled my eyes at Rochelle over my mother's shoulder. Rochelle smiled and shrugged. She was obviously just along for the ride with the tornado that was my mother. I detangled myself from my mom and stepped back, allowing her and Rochelle into the entry. Mom walked past me, ready to take charge, grabbing plates from the kitchen and then settling in the living room. I followed her like a lost puppy.

Once she had the food set out, she settled back and crossed her legs. My mother was slim and didn't look anywhere near her real age. Her stylish sundress showed off her tanned legs and toned arms, which were now crossed and resting on her stomach. Her body language was clear—she was not happy. Rochelle busied herself with a taco, trying to stay out of my mother's way.

"So, tell me what that little shit said."

I sighed heavily and repeated the same story I had told Tracy that morning.

"His skydiving instructor? Are you serious?"

"Why does everyone keep asking me if I'm serious?" I said, grabbing a burrito and dousing it with hot sauce.

"Because it's the most moronic thing I can imagine."

"They're getting married in Mexico? Where in Mexico?" asked Rochelle, between bites of her taco. She and Mom exchanged a look between them, and I immediately knew something was up.

My gaze bounced from Rochelle to my mom as I swallowed my bite of burrito. "I really don't know where. Silly me, I assumed I'd find out when my hand engraved invitation came in the mail."

"Fair enough," mumbled Rochelle.

"Well, ironically, me and Rochelle have a plan. And before you say no, just hear me out," said my mother, her gaze piercing right through me.

Here it comes. I knew they were up to something. When I didn't respond, she continued.

"You know, Rochelle goes on a lot of cruises," said my mom. Rochelle nodded vigorously in agreement. "She meets a lot of very nice people, and it's highly relaxing. We've booked a cruise to Mexico in three weeks, and we think you should come with us. It's just what you need. A change of scenery. And then that little asshole can come and get all his things while you're gone, and you won't even have to see him again."

"A cruise? To Mexico? No. No way. That is *so* not my thing. And I am certainly not going to Mexico. First of all, that's where Brian is getting married. Second, do you know how many food-borne illnesses are contracted there by tourists each year? And cruise ships are notorious for spreading illness. Plus, I really don't like the idea of being on a boat with my bedroom underwater. Thanks, but no thanks."

"We have balcony staterooms," said Rochelle. "You can stay in your mom's room. It sleeps two. You just need a ticket."

I glared at her and she went back to concentrating on her taco.

"Well, Mexico is a big country, Megan. I'm sure we won't run into Brian while we're there. And you can get food poisoning anywhere, so that's certainly not a valid reason to pass up a luxury vacation. You're going to have to do better than that. Besides, I'll get your ticket for you, honey. It will be my treat," said my mom, clearly thinking the matter was settled.

"I don't want to go, Mom. I have work, and it's not a good time."

"It's the best time, Megan. Brian said he was leaving because you were afraid and boring. Prove him wrong. Think of this as a cruise to forget. Forget his name, forget what a lying little prick he is, and forget you wasted three years on him."

Ouch. Shots fired. Guess she was saving that for the punchline.

Prove him wrong. A cruise to forget.

I had to give her credit. She knew me well enough to know that would light a fire in me.

"Why don't you tell me how you really feel, Mom?" I replied, rolling my eyes.

"You know I'm right, sweetheart. Moping around this empty house with reminders of him everywhere isn't going to help you move on."

"I'll think about it," I conceded.

"There's nothing to think about, Megan. You need a change of scenery."

I knew better than to tell her I would think about it. I don't know why I said it. That was all my mother needed to hear. She turned to Rochelle to confirm plans, ignoring that I was sitting right there. The next hour was spent with me protesting and reminding my mom that I said I would *think* about it. I might as well have been talking to the wall. We weren't in a full-on war, but we continued to exchange friendly fire over our Taco Bell feast. I would have enjoyed the fast-food treat and the company, minus the lecture on how I should live my life.

By the time my mom and Rochelle left, I was ready to drop. Arguing with my mother once she had her mind made up about something was an exercise in futility, and I cursed myself again for allowing her an opening. I locked the house up, gathered up the remains of the Taco Bell, and then collapsed on my bed with the TV on, angry at myself for not standing my ground with my mother. The very last thing I wanted to do was to go on a cruise to Mexico.

I should have listened to the little voice in my head that screamed at me not to go. But since that little voice was always screaming at me to avoid doing something, I ignored it.

Spoiler alert. That might have been the one and only time that little voice was right.

CHAPTER FIVE

Megan

The days flew by in a blur, and before I knew it, the weekend loomed ahead of me. I had as much enthusiasm for it as I would for a root canal with no anesthesia. As with most people, I typically couldn't wait for the weekend. That was when Brian and I usually had some much-needed downtime, just the two of us. Instead, I casually scrolled through the persistent barrage of text messages from my mother about the cruise she assumed was a done deal. The pictures she sent did nothing to spark any interest in me. I longed for my previous life. Brian and me, with our whole lives stretched out before us, the two of us enjoying a lazy Saturday morning. Obviously, that ship had sailed. No pun intended.

I spent a few hours puttering around the house on Saturday morning before I couldn't stand being cooped up any longer. It was a beautiful day, so I called Tracy and we made plans to have lunch and do a bit of shopping. I figured some retail therapy was just what I needed, and I loved her for saying yes to my invitation. Tracy was married and had two young children under five years old, so I knew it was no small feat for her to make last-minute plans with me. I told myself I was doing her a favor by whisking her away from a busy morning of sibling fighting and husband nagging. But the truth was,

I'd trade places with her in a heartbeat. I longed for my own family and now that loomed somewhere in the distant future, if ever.

I jumped into the shower and then dressed in a sleeveless sundress in a colorful flower print. If I couldn't exactly *feel* happy, then at least my clothing would convey an upbeat impression to the world.

Tracy chose a restaurant, and we planned to meet at a cozy café in downtown Newport Beach, which offered outdoor seating beside the sidewalk overlooking the beach. My bestie was really making the most of her time away from home. The restaurant was a mix of Paris bistro and California surf vibes, and the combination of the ocean view, the delicious food, and interesting people at the beach made for a great lunch. I enjoyed the cooling ocean breeze while the California sun warmed my bare shoulders, and after lunch we decided to take a stroll along the boardwalk before diving into some serious shopping at nearby South Coast Plaza.

As I stood up and slung my purse over my shoulder, I caught Tracy glaring at something or someone behind me. I turned and scanned the crowded sidewalk. When I spotted Brian, our eyes locked and my stomach did a somersault.

Oh no. It was too soon. I wasn't ready to see him out and about in the wild yet.

He maneuvered through the crowd, heading straight for us. Then I saw *her*. Her was Leticia. Somehow, I knew it was Leticia without actually *knowing* it was Leticia. It wasn't as if my deductive skills were off the chart or anything like that. I mean, it was so obvious. God. It was almost comical how possessive her body language was. If she was a dog, she would have peed on him to mark her territory.

Oh, come on, Universe! Not only did you place him directly in my path, but I have to see her too? Tracy refocused her attention on me and leaned in closer.

"Come on, Megan. Maybe they didn't see us."

Oh, they saw us. No question about it. I was one hundred percent focused on Brian, rooted to the sidewalk. His gaze remained fixed on me. I wanted to look away. I wanted to turn and run in the opposite direction. But I couldn't. I found it impossible to look away from him. And I hated that I was unable to. Instead, I stood there like an idiot, waiting to be humiliated. Leticia noticed him staring at me and nudged him with her elbow. He broke eye contact with me and leaned down to say something to her. He was behaving like a well-trained canine. It was pathetic. They continued walking toward us, and I groaned inwardly. At least I had on my happy dress.

They stopped in front of us, Brian looking as uncomfortable as I did. Neither of us was sure what to do. His arm candy smiled and looked to be all of maybe twenty-one years old. How predictable. She sported bright-pink yoga pants, and a white, cropped, designer t-shirt with Skechers, and probably weighed one-hundred-twenty pounds soaking wet. I was momentarily distracted by the tug-of-war happening with her fashion sense. It was impressive. And not in a good way. From the neck down, she appeared to be out on a casual day of errands. But her face looked like it was headed to the Met Gala she was so heavily made up. Just to clarify, I wasn't bitter at all. My thoughts were nothing more than the simple observation of the she-devil my ex had taken up with.

The irony of it was that Leticia was just the type of woman Brian and I always made fun of. A Karen-in-training, he called them. He used to say he couldn't stand that type, that they made him sick. But looking at him now, he sure didn't look like he was going to be sick anytime soon.

As I feigned fascination with the sidewalk, gazing down at it as if it held the key to my ex-fiancé quandary, the flowers on my happy dress practically wilted right off me. I genuinely wished the ground would just open up and swallow me whole. It would be less painful than standing there watching Brian slide his arm around Leticia's Barbie-sized waist with such intimate familiarity.

"Hey," said Brian.

Tracy glared at him.

"Um, hi," was my less than brilliant response. *Someone shoot me now and put me out of my misery, please.*

"Letty, this is Megan. And her friend, Tracy."

Letty? A nickname so soon? I couldn't help but notice that he was no longer using *my* nickname when he introduced us. Letty stared at us, utterly clueless.

"Oh, hey. So how do you know my fiancé?" she asked, casting a quick look at me and Tracy with a phony smile plastered on her face.

Seriously? I was baffled that she had no idea who I was. Most women would have checked out their future groom's ex-fiancée on social media to learn every detail of her life. Yet, her unwavering stare made it apparent that she was truly oblivious. I wasn't sure how the woman could possibly be any more self-absorbed.

"Megan was engaged to Brian until a week ago. You may have heard about their upcoming wedding that she has to cancel?" scowled Tracy. I could have kissed her for it.

"Oh, seriously? You're *that* Megan? Oh, well, this is awkward," she said, inhaling sharply and tightening her vise-like grip on Brian's arm.

She fluttered her over-the-top false eyelashes and then had the audacity to give me a once-over before she averted her gaze dismissively, totally uninterested in me. She was completely confident that she had nothing to worry about. Brian belonged to her now, and she had no qualms about making sure I understood that. I wanted to rip her fake lashes off and scratch her eyes out. Tracy must have sensed my rage because she hurriedly grabbed my arm and guided me farther down the sidewalk before I could lunge at Leticia. In doing so, she also rescued me from a full-blown panic attack. I didn't resist Tracy's efforts because I was certain if I stayed there even one second longer, I was definitely going to lose control and pounce on Brian's future child bride.

I let Tracy pull me along without looking back. We ducked into a nearby surf shop, snatched a couple of random bathing suits from a rack by the door, and made our way to the fitting rooms. I slumped onto the bench, feeling totally numb.

"Are you okay?" she asked me.

"I, um, she. . ." I was struggling to string together a coherent sentence.

"She is a frigging house plant, Megan. Did she really just say *awkward* when introduced to you? The girl has no shame. What is Brian thinking? My God, what is she, like, thirteen? He'll have to learn all the latest teenage slang and memorize the words to all of Taylor Swift's songs now just to have a viable conversation with her."

I couldn't stop myself from laughing. Then I burst into sobs because it felt like a natural transition. What else was I supposed to do? Leticia was obviously younger than me. I had to concede she was prettier, or rather she would be, without all the makeup. And she had the confidence and the body to wear a crop top in public.

A crop top! In public!

She was, without a doubt, a monster. I sniffed and accepted the tissue Tracy produced from her purse, even though it had half a cough drop stuck to one end of it.

"Yeah. She *is* a houseplant. And he's a tool. And what was up with those eyelashes of hers? She can't believe anyone thinks those are real, right? It looked like a couple of tarantulas planted themselves on her eyelids. What an insult that he left me for *her*," I lamented between sobs.

"Atta girl. Get it all out," said Tracy, using a soothing voice while gently patting my back.

I sighed and stared at the floor. "And on top of everything else, my mom wants me to go on a cruise with her and Rochelle to Mexico in two weeks. She thinks I need a change of scenery. She won't stop talking about it, and she bought me a ticket. So now I feel obligated to go," I complained, thinking Tracy would sympathize with my plight. I figured I might as well lay all my problems out on the table for her to dissect in one sitting.

"Well, if I didn't already know your mother, I'd say she sounds awful," she said, rolling her eyes. "Imagine trying to do something nice, like whisking her daughter off to an all-expenses paid cruise. That woman has got some nerve."

Okay, obviously, Tracy was not team Megan when it came to the upcoming cruise. My one and only ally was breaking rank with me. The day just kept getting better.

Once I had cried myself out, I dried my eyes and stood up, feeling more ready than ever for some retail therapy. American Express was going to love me this month.

I arrived home late that afternoon and headed straight for the Ben & Jerry's, which I had already replaced once in the past week. By eight o'clock, I had dozed off on the couch, surrounded by an empty pint of ice cream and a half-empty bottle of wine on the coffee table.

Yet another amazing day for me. *Not.*

CHAPTER SIX

Megan

If you've never experienced your overly involved mother guilt-tripping you into a vacation, I don't recommend it. In fact, I urge you to avoid it no matter what.

My mother relentlessly refused to give up on the cruise idea. Without fail, she called me every day after work to give me yet another reason why I would love our upcoming vacation. She actually suggested I get a language app to learn Spanish and then incorporate one or two new words per day into conversation as preparation. That came dangerously close to being the breaking point for me. I knew she meant well, but honestly, she was driving me crazy.

Tracy was no help either. She repeatedly encouraged me to relax and enjoy myself, for once. *Relaxing.* I'd heard of it, of course. I realized it was something that other people did regularly. It just wasn't something I was very familiar with.

It was the week before the cruise, and time was dragging by. My vacation request at work had been approved, and the substitute teacher was booked. My mother dropped off my ticket, which sealed the deal. I had exhausted all my excuses. Tracy suggested I buy a couple of outfits for the cruise on our recent shopping trip, and I picked up an evening gown I had to admit looked pretty good on me.

The one positive thing I could say about the cruise was that I looked forward to wearing my new dress.

With a gaping hole in my life now that Brian was gone and nothing else to occupy my time, I jumped headfirst down the research rabbit hole when I googled cruises. Because that's what I always did. I wanted to ensure I was well informed. Tracy compared me to a hypochondriac trolling WebMD. My motto was to be educated and prepared, which was why I ignored her. I didn't see any problem with wanting to know what I was dealing with. However, after completing the research, I regretted it.

The initial phase of my search was innocuous. I learned that about three hundred ships operated by over fifty cruise lines carried 13.9 million passengers visiting over two hundred ports every year. North America accounted for about half of those passengers. Nothing to set off any alarm bells yet. Fire posed the greatest threat to passengers, statistically. I was okay with that since we would be surrounded by water and lifeboats. Which was to say that didn't completely freak me out. Violent crime rates decreased by ninety-five percent on water compared to land. So that was good to hear.

After that, I started focusing on the other statistics. And that's when things started to unravel for me. Out of the 13.9 million passengers annually, 1,940 of them fell ill. Sick enough to visit the onboard doctor or hospital. That was a lot of sick people when you really considered the number. That was an entire Midwest small town. I realized that cruise ships were essentially floating petri dishes. I made a mental note to myself to get a flu shot and pack some Emergen-C for the trip.

But it was the last thing I found out that sent me into a minor tailspin. Every year, two-hundred people vanished without a trace from cruise ships. When I shared that statistic with Tracy, she dismissed my concerns as being ridiculous and paranoid, pointing out that it was a negligible percentage of travelers. I disagreed. Two-hundred lives were equivalent to roughly seven of my classrooms, and the mystery of what happened to all those people would likely never be solved. I couldn't be the only person who thought that number was shocking. Did those people fall overboard? Did they go missing while in port in a foreign country? It was a terrifying thought. I tried not to obsess over it, however the thought kept resurfacing. But it was too late to change my mind about going on the cruise now, anyway. There was no way my mom would let me skip it without making me regret it every day for the rest of my life.

A couple of days went by, and I was down in the dumps, facing another weekend ahead with no plans. I hesitated to ask Tracy to do anything, especially after the disaster we experienced last weekend. I was puttering around the house, doing some light cleaning on Saturday morning, when the doorbell rang. I assumed it was probably my mom, dropping off another outfit for the cruise. Earlier in the week, she had already left a bathing suit, shorts, and a couple of casual day dresses. Even though I kept telling her I didn't need any more clothes for the trip. Despite her generous intentions, her efforts to help felt a little suffocating. But I had learned years ago to pick my battles with my mother, and a few pieces of clothing were hardly battle-worthy.

I flung the front door open, expecting to see my mom there, but instead, Brian stood leaning against the stucco wall with two large suitcases at his side. My hand instinctively moved to my hair; a messy bun held in place with a couple of strategically placed bobby pins. Great. I glanced at the suitcases and felt my heart lurch. Did he come to beg me to let him come home?

"Hey, Megan. I thought maybe I could pick up the rest of my clothes and stuff. Is this a bad time?" he asked, gazing at my sweatpants and Talking Heads t-shirt. A far cry from hot pink yoga pants and a crop top.

Of course, he wasn't coming back. He was finishing his packing. I looked at him for a second, trying to figure out whether the two weeks spent apart had improved my attitude, and therefore my opinion of him. The answer to that was not even a little bit.

Big. Fat. *Nada.*

Well, at least my mother would be proud of me. I had used my one Spanish word today. I stepped aside and pulled the front door open, allowing him inside. Then I peered outside to make sure he was alone before shutting the door. At least he had the decency not to bring his adolescent concubine with him.

I gestured for him to head to the bedroom and then I sank onto the couch. As soon as he disappeared down the hall, I sprang up and darted into the bathroom. I let out a groan when I saw my reflection in the mirror. I finger-combed my hair and let it cascade around my face, pinching my cheeks to give myself a hint of color. It was the best I could do, given the circumstances.

Back out in the living room, I busied myself on my phone until Brian emerged thirty minutes later. He rolled the suitcases to the door and took a seat in the chair opposite me.

"I think I got everything. How are you doing? Are you okay?"

I was furious that he believed I couldn't manage without him. Did he think he was so amazing that I would just downright crumble when he left? I told myself it wasn't necessary for him to know about my nightly blubbering over him. And there was no way I was going to let him see how broken I really was. The pity in his eyes pushed me to my breaking point.

"Listen, Brian, what's done is done. Honestly, I'm sick of thinking about it. I am *exhausted* thinking about it, actually. You may have some more gas to regurgitate the situation, but frankly, I'm out of steam." *Take that, you cheating jerk.*

"I'm glad you're okay, Megs. I've been worried about you. I wasn't sure how you would handle this."

Oof. He had some nerve calling me Megs. As if we were still on a nickname basis. We weren't. He was engaged to someone else now. Plus, the thought of him thinking I was alone and going to pieces over him made my blood boil.

"I'm fine. Brilliant, actually. In fact, I'm going on a cruise next week." I hadn't intended to blurt that out, and I immediately regretted it. It sounded like I was trying to convince him I was okay.

Which was, of course, exactly what I was doing. I just didn't need him to know that.

"Great! I'm glad you're finally getting out there to do something fun. It will do you good to get away," he said cheerily, but sympathy was written all over his expression.

"Yeah, it should be a lot of fun," I muttered, without meeting his gaze.

"I'll be out of town starting next week as well. Where are you cruising to?"

"Uh, Mexico. You out of town for work then?"

"No. Actually, Letty and I moved the wedding date up. I'll be in Costa Maya."

What?

There it was. The kill shot. He might not have meant it to be, but it was a crushing blow. After a quick mental calculation, I realized we would be in Mexico at the same time, only about a hundred miles apart. Brian at his dream destination wedding in Costa Maya, and me on my nightmare cruise to Playa del Carmen. Lovely. The Brian-sized hole in my heart widened as my mind raced, once again desperately searching for excuses to get out of going on the cruise.

I was still lost in thought when Brian stood up to leave. I walked him to the door and watched his departing figure as he loaded the luggage onto the back of his truck bed and climbed into the cab. Then he drove his truck away from the life we built together. The life we once shared. I watched until he disappeared down the street, back to his new, perfect life. I stood on my porch and wept as I reflected on the disaster my world had suddenly become.

CHAPTER SEVEN

Megan

I woke up on the morning of the cruise, replaying my final conversation with Brian in my head. I whimpered, remembering I was single now. *Single.* I tested the word out in my mind. I hated it.

There was so much more I wanted to say to Brian, and now I would never get the chance. Part of me knew we would probably never speak again, and the thought of that tore me apart. I felt pathetic. I had been awake for exactly three minutes and I was already falling apart. Blinking back the waterworks, I forced myself out of bed.

Despite feeling fairly well-rested, I still lacked any enthusiasm for the cruise. I tried to get myself psyched up for the trip over the last couple of days, but my reluctance remained. My world was very me-centric. I stayed in my comfort zone and didn't venture far from it. I was also not the most insightful person. I had settled into a rhythm of work and wedding planning and now that half of that equation had been ripped from me, I felt lost. Going on a cruise I was already apprehensive about wasn't helping that.

Still, I went through the motions and jumped into the shower. I decided on jeans and a flowy top that concealed the extra five pounds I had packed on from my three-week Ben & Jerry's ice cream binge. Cruises were known for their decadent food, so this vacation was going to do nothing to help take that extra weight off. I told myself I would eat only healthy meals on the cruise. Right. Because, of course, that was going to happen.

By the time I got my luggage to the living room, my mom was already ringing my doorbell. I braced myself and took a deep breath while I mentally prepared for the enthusiastic bundle of joy waiting for me on my porch.

As I swung the door open, my mom let out a squeal. I genuinely tried my best not to smile. I wanted her to know that I wasn't happy about my enforced vacation. But her excitement was contagious, and she was obviously thrilled that I was going on the cruise with her. She pulled me into a hug, squeezing me tightly.

"Oh, honey, I'm so happy you're coming with us! You're going to love it, I promise. A cruise to forget!"

"Yeah, right," I sighed, smiling at her and grabbing my suitcase.

I peered around her toward the porch. "Where's Rochelle?"

"Oh, she's meeting us there."

"Really? That's weird. I figured we'd all be going together."

"Oh, she always does this. She's a control freak and wants to make sure everything is taken care of. Besides, this will give us some time alone to talk. Have you heard from Brian?"

"Mother, please. The last thing I want to talk about is Brian. Let's just consider him, or any topics that involve him, off limits. Okay?"

"That's my girl," she said, beaming at me.

She stepped back onto the porch, and I followed her, locking the door behind me. I glanced back at my house one final time, feeling as if I were on a walk to my own execution.

What was wrong with me? Why was I unable to have fun on vacation or appreciate anything even remotely enjoyable, like a normal person? In that instant, I vowed to give the vacation a fair shot, no matter what. I would try to release my inhibitions and unwind.

I repeated the same pep talk to myself all the way to San Pedro, to the Port of Los Angeles. I thought I was doing fine and was actually on the verge of convincing myself. Right up until we pulled into the World Cruise Center parking lot.

"Ready, Megan?"

I sat staring straight ahead and made no move to unbuckle my seat belt. It was my last chance to get out of going. Once I stepped outside of the car, that would be it. I would be committed.

"Come on, Megan. You're going to love this cruise. I promise."

Not likely. I would probably love it about as much as I would a frontal lobotomy. I could see my mother staring at me in my peripheral vision, willing me to get out of the car. With a sigh, I pressed the button to release my seatbelt. The belt retracted swiftly, leaving me no opportunity for second thoughts. My mom actually clapped her hands she was so excited. I practiced my deep breathing technique as we got our luggage out of the trunk and was proud of myself for remaining calm as we started toward the boarding area.

That all changed when I laid eyes on the ship.

We walked side by side toward the massive vessel, my mom chatting excitedly the entire time. The *Jewel of the Sea* towered a staggering fifteen decks high and was an imposing sight from below. Thoughts of the Titanic kept popping into my head. My heart jumped wildly in my chest as I gazed upwards, stunned by its sheer magnitude.

"I know it looks monstrous from down here, but trust me, once we are on board, it doesn't feel that way."

Sure. I gripped the handle of my luggage, determined not to give in to my panic. My thoughts were consumed by all the things that could go wrong. *Fire. Illness. Falling overboard. Disappearing without a trace.* I took a shallow breath just to reassure myself that I could still breathe on my own.

I once again mentally chastised myself for researching cruises. I knew I would become fixated on the bad things and drive myself crazy. But it didn't stop me from doing it, leaving no one but myself to blame for my current state of anxiety. Part of me wanted to voice my concerns to my mom because I knew she would try to reassure me and tell me I was being ridiculous. The more practical side of me knew neither of us was prepared to take that deep dive into my psyche. Instead, I steadied my breathing and pressed on toward the ship, my mom's constant chatter in my ear.

After arriving at the cruise terminal, we waited no more than thirty minutes until our group was cleared to board. It was a welcome distraction to have something to focus on rather than waiting around while my uneasiness grew. Mom already had our boarding documents and passports ready. Normally, it would annoy me if she asked for my passport, suggesting I was incapable of getting through security on my own. But I was thankful for her taking charge while I focused on calming down. She insisted she use her credit card for onboard purchases, despite my protests. Cruises are cashless vacations, and she assured me she could afford to treat me. A kindergarten teacher's salary wasn't exactly lavish, so I was grateful for her generosity.

After checking in, we gave our luggage to the porters to deliver to our cabin later. Going through security wasn't nearly as rigorous as it was at an airport, and I was beginning to feel more relaxed. Then we were required to complete a form regarding recent illnesses, and of course, my worries came rushing back. Once we passed security, we had our pictures taken, and received our cruise cards, which served as our ship's ID, room key, boarding card, and onboard credit card. I had no clue all of that was needed. I had pictured us walking up the plank and straight on board, just like in the movies. We didn't reach the gangway until after the photographers along the way confirmed we didn't want any memory photos.

No thanks. I didn't need to remember the feeling of dread that made my stomach churn.

We milled about the main atrium, which was abuzz with excited guests and smiling staff serving cocktails. I hastily grabbed a glass of champagne to help settle my nerves. Two glasses later, I was swaying to the live band and sampling some of the finger foods. It wasn't long before our room category was cleared and we were off. My mom and

Rochelle made plans for us to meet in our room once we were checked in, so we made our way to the cabin.

Our stateroom was comfortable with two queen beds, a couch and chair, a full bathroom, and a small balcony that would offer a stunning view once we were at sea. Not that I had any intention of setting foot on the balcony. We were on one of the upper cabin decks, and I honestly didn't want to know how high up we were, especially after seeing the size of the ship we were on. I had never been a fan of heights. At all.

My plan was to spend much of my time in the room reading, anyway. The sliding door in the room prevented it from feeling claustrophobic, allowing me to imagine myself catching up on my reading list and getting lost in a good book.

However, life has a knack for throwing obstacles your way. And even though I had misgivings about the trip, I had no clue that something unimaginable would happen to me while I was on the ship. If I had known what was coming, I might have had the courage to leap from the balcony back onto solid ground.

CHAPTER EIGHT

Megan

Shortly after we arrived in our room, the porter delivered our luggage. I placed my suitcase on the bed and sat down beside it, preparing to unpack.

"Megan, leave the unpacking for later. Let's order drinks and sit on the balcony while we wait for Rochelle. Then we can head out to the pool deck and get some sun for our first day at sea."

I glanced up at my mom, who was busy checking her makeup and hair in the vanity mirror. "No thanks, Mom. I'm just going to get settled and catch up on some reading. That champagne made me a little sleepy," I responded wearily, yawning as if to prove my point.

The look of surprise on my mother's face spoke volumes, but her obvious state of shock wasn't enough to render her silent. "Oh, for heaven's sake. You can read at home. You're on a *cruise,* Megan. I didn't buy you a ticket so you could hide out in the room the entire time. Don't be ridiculous. Throw on that new bathing suit I got you and grab a cover-up. I'm not taking no for an answer."

She stood with her hands on her hips and her head cocked to the side. Her firm stance confirmed her unwillingness to compromise, and I got the message loud and clear. I glanced longingly at the books stuffed into the netting of my suitcase, but my mom pulled my new bathing suit out and tossed it to me.

"C'mon, Megan. Have a cocktail with your mother. We're on vacation, for goodness' sakes. Remember, you're on a cruise to for—"

"I know, Mom. A cruise to forget. I've heard your tagline enough times. You can stop now."

It was easier to give in rather than argue, so I pulled my cover-up from under the pile of clothes in my suitcase and strode toward the bathroom. The thought of putting on my bikini filled me with dread, because I felt self-conscious about the weight I had gained after using Ben & Jerry's as a crutch during my breakup. Even though I knew I would likely never cross paths with anyone on the cruise again, I still felt a little embarrassed. Still, my mother was unfamiliar with the concept of no and seldom accepted failure.

After changing, I joined my mom on the balcony, dragging my chair as far away from the edge as possible. She gave me an exasperated look that I chose to ignore. I closed my eyes, breathing in the salty air while we waited for room service to deliver our cocktails. I was on the verge of drifting off when a sharp knock at the door brought me fully awake.

"I'll get it," said Mom, springing up from her chair.

I turned to see Rochelle enter the room, dressed in her swimsuit and cover-up, and carrying a straw bag. Before she could reach the balcony, there was another knock on the door and our drinks arrived. I grabbed my Long Island Iced Tea and downed a good portion of it before stuffing sunscreen, lip balm, and a towel into my beach bag.

Rochelle pulled me into a hello hug and moments later, we were on our way out of the room. Even though the pool deck was already crowded, we lucked out and found three lounge chairs grouped together near the bar. Despite being in direct sunlight on the deck, the proximity of our seats to the bar was a good trade-off. If I was going to survive this cruise, I would need drinks. Lots of them. From my perspective, the struggle was undeniably real.

After settling into our loungers poolside, Rochelle and my mom kept up a steady stream of chatter about all the things they had planned for us on our trip. I only half-listened to them as I was preoccupied with people watching. My sunglasses offered me a way to check out the other passengers discreetly, without being distasteful about it. Occasionally, I chimed into the conversation to make my mom believe I was paying attention, but truthfully, my focus was on an attractive man at the bar. The cuffs of his white shirt were rolled up to reveal chiseled forearms. Chuckling at something the bartender said, he leisurely sipped his beer while relaxing on the barstool. I quickly looked away when he glanced at me, hoping he didn't notice the blush on my cheeks. When I turned around again, he was leaning toward a woman in the adjacent seat, exuding charm that was obvious even from where I sat. There was no question he was a player. It was just as well, I thought to myself. I had no business thinking about men. At that very moment, my ex-fiancé was probably with his new bride-to-be on the way to their wedding destination. I breathed in deeply, refusing to let myself shed any more tears over Brian. Instead, I indulged in another long sip from my cocktail, allowing the alcohol to help blur the memories.

As I leaned back in the chair and was about to close my eyes, a roar erupted from the crowd, causing me to sit up and investigate. On the opposite end of the deck, a small band had set up, filling the air with music. Both my mom and Rochelle, along with a crowd of people around us, jumped to their feet and started dancing to the popular song. Reaching down, my mom grasped my hand and urged me to join them. I shook my head and pulled away, taking another sizeable gulp of my cocktail, then laid my head back and shut my eyes. A few seconds later, a shadow fell over me, shielding me from the sun. I opened one eye and peeked through my sunglasses to see who was blocking my rays. I sat up and removed my glasses, only to find myself staring at the handsome man from the bar.

"Good afternoon. May I have the honor?" he questioned, holding out his hand to me.

It took a second for me to realize he was asking me to dance. I glanced over at my mom, who was beaming at me and motioning for me to stand. I shot her a stern look, hoping she would get the message to mind her own business. A smile played on the lips of the mystery man as he raised his eyebrows in question. What the hell. What harm could a dance with him do? Old Megan would have instantly rejected his invitation without a second thought. New Megan accepted before I could reconsider. I laid my hand in his and smiled as he lifted me off the chair.

There was a minute of silence as we swayed to the music. Thankfully, the cocktail I had guzzled down in two sips was boosting my courage.

"I'm Nate Talbert," he said, pulling back to look at me, but not letting go.

"Megan Hamilton," I responded.

His eyes were the color of the ocean, and I was equally mesmerized and intimidated. His gaze was laser focused on me, and while some women might find that attentive, I found it unnerving.

"Well, Megan Hamilton, it's a pleasure to meet you."

"Likewise, Nate Talbert."

The flow of alcohol continued to calm my inhibitions, and we spent hours on deck, dancing, eating, and drinking. My mom and Rochelle gave us our space, only joining us when Nate insisted on it. The conversation with Nate was effortless, and I found him to be intelligent and charming. He provided a pleasant distraction from me obsessing over Brian getting married sometime over the weekend, just a few miles from where our ship would dock in Playa del Carmen. While Brian crossed my mind multiple times throughout the day, I swiftly pushed any thoughts of him out of my head. I was proud of my progress, considering I was still crying myself to sleep over him a week ago. I hated to admit it, but maybe my mom was right. Maybe the cruise was exactly what I needed to get over Brian.

Midafternoon arrived, and I collapsed onto my lounge chair, utterly exhausted from the combination of the sun, the drinks, and dancing. Nate took the seat next to mine and glanced over at me, laughing.

"Thank you, Megan. I haven't had this much fun in a very long time."

"Ditto. I was actually dreading this vacation, to be totally honest. But I really am having a good time. Thank you for that. I needed this," I said.

"You were dreading this cruise? Why?" he asked, a puzzled look on his face.

"I don't know. This kind of thing just truthfully isn't in my wheelhouse. Traveling to a foreign country. Trapped on a ship in the ocean." I glanced at my mother at the bar. "Vacationing with my mother," I stated, leaning closer to him and lowering my voice.

"Well, I can relate to vacationing with a parent. I've been there, done that," he joked. "But I don't get the other issues. Mexico is beautiful. And we will hardly be in the middle of the ocean. We will probably be able to see land for most of the cruise."

"I realize it sounds ridiculous. But I'm sort of a cautious person. Not very adventurous. My ex called me boring recently. And I'm afraid he was right. So I'm trying to broaden my horizons a bit. This cruise is the first step to a new me."

"Well, personally, I think your ex sounds like a buffoon. You are anything but boring, Megan. I find you absolutely delightful and very beautiful."

I don't care who you are. Being called beautiful never gets old. Especially when you've just been dumped.

"Buffoon, huh? That's a word you don't hear often. And thank you, by the way. I've had a wonderful day."

"It doesn't have to end, you know. Spend the evening with me tonight. We can grab some dinner, see a show, maybe stop by one of the casinos."

I studied Nate's face. I couldn't seem to take my eyes off him. Was this handsome man actually interested in spending more time with me? My self-esteem took a hit after the breakup with Brian, and it had left me doubting myself. Nate's smile widened as he tilted his head at me, eager for an answer.

"We have to eat, right?" I said, smiling back at him.

"Not the most romantic response I've ever had to a dinner invitation, but I'll take it," he chuckled.

I found myself unable to stop smiling as the warm sunshine, the ocean breeze, and the effortless conversation with Nate all competed for my attention. I let my head rest against the back of the chair, and for the first time in a long while, I surrendered and simply let life unfold as it pleased, embracing the unknown. I was certainly on a roll as the new me.

I felt hopeful for the first time in three weeks. It was easily an improvement over being home alone, obsessing over my failed relationship with a fiancé who no longer loved me.

CHAPTER NINE

Megan

I slipped into my cocktail dress and admired my reflection in the mirror, turning to see myself from every angle. My hair hung loose in soft waves that framed my face. My complexion radiated a healthy glow from the afternoon sun, while my earrings shimmered against my dark hair.

"Megan, you look absolutely beautiful," said my mom, smiling at me from the couch.

"Thanks, Mom. I feel beautiful."

"So, what are you two getting up to tonight?"

"I'm not sure, really. He mentioned dinner, maybe a casino or a show. I let him plan the date."

"How exciting, honey. Rochelle and I will stay out of your way, I promise."

"Mom, there are literally thousands of people on this ship. I doubt I could find you two tonight even if I was looking," I replied, laughing.

"Well, I'm just saying, if we see you, we will turn heel and skedaddle."

"Okay. You *skedaddle* then, if you see us. That's a plan," I said, internally rolling my eyes at her statement.

A knock at the door saved me from any more awkward conversation with her. When I opened the door, Nate stood there looking striking in a perfectly tailored white dress shirt, black dress slacks and the most mesmerizing blue eyes I had ever seen.

"Wow, Megan. You look stunning," he breathed, leaning in to kiss my cheek.

I felt the heat flush my face. "You look very nice as well, Nate."

"You two are a lovely couple. Let me take a picture before you leave," said my mom, rummaging through her purse for her phone.

Oh. My. God. It was prom night all over again. Only worse. Shaking my head, I let my chin fall to my chest. Nate noticed my body language, and being the perfect gentleman, came to my rescue.

"You know, Michelle, sadly, I don't think we have time. We have dinner reservations, and these restaurants are sticklers about punctuality. But I promise to take some pictures for you this evening and send them to you tomorrow."

That satisfied my mother enough to prevent her from dumping her entire purse on the bed. I mouthed "thank you" to Nate, and he responded with a smile and a wink. We made a hasty exit before my mother could start lecturing us about safe sex or something equally embarrassing. As we walked down the long corridor, Nate reached over and gently took my hand in his.

I turned to look at him. "Is this okay?" he asked, holding up our entwined hands.

I smiled and squeezed his hand in return. It was more than just okay.

"I'm sorry about my mother. She means well, but she can be a tad much at times. I'm her only child, and since my dad passed when I was young, she feels this overwhelming need to protect me and be involved in every single detail of my life."

"Don't worry about it. I think she's great. You're lucky to have a parent who cares so much about you. Mine are both gone, and I miss them terribly."

"I'm so sorry. I didn't mean to dredge up a bad memory for you."

"Not at all. They passed away several years ago in a plane crash. It's nice to talk about them once in a while. It keeps their memory alive."

We continued with our casual conversation as we navigated the ship. Nate seemed to know where he was going and I followed along, just happy to be spending time with him. Instead of going to the main dining room as I expected, he took me to a specialty restaurant. It was gorgeous and first-class and I felt like a princess.

The maître d' seated us in a secluded corner, where a candlelit table awaited us, and Nate selected a bottle of Château Mouton Rothschild 2022. The waiter seemed impressed by Nate's selection, which I assumed was pricey since I had never heard of it. I was accustomed to drinking inexpensive wine from Trader Joe's and I was perfectly content with that. I wasn't someone who got hung up on labels. Besides, Charles Shaw's wine, famously known as two-buck-chuck, was pretty good. But the wine that Nate ordered delivered a wholly different experience. By the time we had finished dinner, I was tipsy and giggling like a lovesick teenager.

We left the restaurant holding hands again, and it felt absolutely effortless. Despite that, there was still a constant voice in my head telling me it was too soon. That I needed to take things at a slower pace. However, the new me came out on top of that argument, and for once, I mustered the courage to overcome my fear and take a leap of faith.

We decided to go to one of the casinos to kill some time before our ten o'clock show began. I hadn't spent much time in a casino before then, but the atmosphere was intoxicating. Maybe the appeal was the potential to win money. Or maybe it was Nate's company. Whatever it was, I was drunk on life at that point.

Despite not needing it, I still drank the wine Nate ordered me. By the time we sat down for the show, I was already so infatuated with Nate that I didn't resist when he leaned in to kiss me in the dimly lit theater. I felt an electric shock course through my body at the touch of his lips against mine. That was far from ordinary and I was fully aware of it and I was utterly captivated. From the moment we shared that first kiss, I knew I was hopelessly hooked. But I didn't care. Maybe my mom was right, and I was genuinely forgetting about my heartbreak.

Brian who?

CHAPTER TEN

Megan

I was on such a high after spending a wonderful evening with Nate last night and hanging out with him at the pool again today. I laid the dress I bought with Tracy for the captain's dinner on the bed, smoothing it out. It was even more impressive than I remembered, and I thought I could learn to like dressing up more often.

"Oh, Megan, you are going to turn heads in that dress," gushed my mom.

"You think so? There's only one head I'm interested in turning," I said, smiling at her.

"Don't take this the wrong way, but do you think you're spending too much time with this new guy? I am all for you moving on from Brian, sweetheart, but you just met him and he has monopolized almost all of your time since we got here. I haven't had any mother-daughter time with you yet. It just seems like overkill to me, that's all."

"His name is Nate, Mom, and I would think you'd be thrilled to see me interested in someone else, especially since the whole point of me coming on this cruise was to move on from Brian." I turned to face her. "Look, I'm having fun, and that's what you wanted me to do, right? Forget and have fun? Well, I am. You can't have it both ways, Mom."

"I just hoped we would be able to spend some more time together, that's all."

I walked toward my ever-fretting mother and pulled her into an embrace. "Mom, I will spend all day with you tomorrow. I promise."

"Really? Because we only have a few more days on the cruise and I'd like to go shopping in Playa del Carmen tomorrow."

"Well, you'll have to go with Rochelle then. Because I have no desire to get off the ship in Mexico," I insisted, returning to the dressing table to put the finishing touches on my makeup.

"Don't be silly, Megan. The entire point of the cruise is to go somewhere. It's perfectly safe. I've done it dozens of times."

"That may be true, but I'm still not getting off the ship. You go shopping with Rochelle in the morning, and I'll catch some more sun at the pool until you get back. I'm sure Nate would be happy to keep me company."

My mom sighed and grabbed her wrap. "Fine. Are you ready?"

I stole one last glance in the mirror, picked up my clutch, and joined her at the door. "Let's go."

We swung by Rochelle's room before making our way to the main dining room for the captain's dinner. Just outside the entrance, Nate stood waiting for us in a black tuxedo. I was so taken aback by his handsomeness that it almost left me breathless.

He smiled as he walked toward us and held out his arm for me. "You look incredible, Megan."

"Ditto."

"Ladies, shall we?" he asked, motioning toward the entrance.

Entering the dining room was like taking a step back in time. The room was reminiscent of something straight out of the 1920s. The ambience was elevated by the exquisite food presentation, sparkling crystal chandeliers, and the delicate clinking of crystal and silver. The room was filled with the gentle hum of voices and laughter, while the scent of fresh flowers floated through the air. Nate chatted with the maître d' while I absorbed everything around me. I'd never been to a more beautifully set dinner, and I was in awe. The steward led us to our table, where we ordered wine and a scallop appetizer. The evening was perfect. After dinner, Nate requested I join him for a dance, and I melted into his arms as if it was where I had always belonged.

Shortly after eleven o'clock, my mom and Rochelle excused themselves, claiming exhaustion from so much afternoon sun. I couldn't ignore the worry on my mom's face, so I pulled her aside.

"What's wrong? I can tell you're worried. You don't need to be, you know. I'm a grown woman."

"I know that, dear. I just don't want you to fall for this guy and then we go back home and you never hear from him again. It would be so easy to get caught up in the romance of it all here on the ship."

"Thanks for your vote of confidence in me, Mom."

"Megan, I didn't mean anything by that. I just don't want you to get hurt. Not after what you've already been through."

"I know, and I get it. I do. But for the first time since Brian left me, I'm happy. So can't you just be happy for me?"

"Yes. Yes, of course I can," she replied, pulling me close. "We'll talk more tomorrow after Rochelle and I get back from Playa del Carmen and our shopping trip. Remember, save the rest of the day for me tomorrow."

"I will. I promise."

Once my mom and Rochelle left for their rooms, I rejoined Nate at the table. Both the conversation and the wine flowed effortlessly, and before I knew it, it was almost 2:00 a.m.

"I'd better get to my room and get some sleep. I'm pretty wiped out, and if I have any more wine, I may sleep until noon tomorrow," I teased.

"You're on vacation. You should indulge yourself and sleep in a little late if you want to. How about a brandy nightcap? It will help you sleep."

"All right. But this is my last drink," I said, narrowing my eyes at him playfully.

"Scout's honor," he promised, rising.

Nate returned to the table a few minutes later, carrying two brandy snifters. I took small sips of my drink, too weary to fully appreciate it, but still reluctant to let the night come to an end. I was falling for him, and that was the last thing I wanted to do. It was way too early and decidedly out of character for me to have developed such intense feelings for him. Plus, I didn't want to complicate my life further by getting tangled up in a rebound relationship, even if it was nothing but a fleeting shipboard romance. I didn't think my heart could take it.

"Let's finish our drinks and I'll walk you back to your room. Down the hatch," motioned Nate, draining his glass.

Doing the same, I suppressed a cough as the alcohol burned my throat. Nate gestured to the waiter for our check while I gathered my things. A few minutes later, Nate signed for the bill, and we were ready to leave. He pulled my chair out for me, and I stood up and swayed unexpectedly. Grabbing my clutch and wrap, I used one hand to steady myself on the table.

Nate caught me, taking hold of my arm. "Hey, are you okay?"

"Yes. I just stood up too fast, I guess. Head rush," I said, shaking my head.

"All right. Let's get you into bed," he prodded, guiding me toward the door.

By the time we reached the hallway, my head was spinning, and I was struggling to walk straight. "I don't feel so great, Nate. I think I need to sit down for a minute." I felt like I was walking through a dense fog, unable to concentrate, and slurring my words.

"No. Let me take you to your room. You just had too much to drink."

Alcohol never impacted me this way. Something was very wrong. Holding onto the railing with one hand, I attempted to free myself from Nate's grasp on my other arm. He held on tightly, and I couldn't understand why he wouldn't allow me to sit down. Just then, a crew member appeared out of nowhere, and Nate whispered something to him. The man grasped my arm as Nate released his hold. He led me forward while Nate turned to leave. The man's face blurred in and out of my vision, distorting his face.

Why was Nate leaving me with this stranger?

"No! Nate, help me," I cried, as the man tightened his grasp on my arm.

Nate spun around and hurriedly walked back to me as I fought to escape the crew member's grip on me.

"Megan, stop it. You are in no condition to fight."

I kicked at the man holding me, still confused about what was happening.

"Are you trying to get yourself thrown overboard? You will do as you're told or you will end up dead. Is that understood?" ordered Nate, grabbing my face and turning it toward him.

The coldness in his eyes made me freeze as fear wound its way up my spine. My mouth moved, but I was rendered speechless by the sudden change in his demeanor. He was right. I was in no condition physically or mentally to fight. My movements were sluggish and uncoordinated, and a horrible uneasiness settled in my stomach as I realized Nate had spiked my drink. The thought literally made me sick, and I leaned over to retch.

Why would Nate drug me? Things were going so well between us, and I couldn't grasp what I knew had to be the truth. I tried to scream for help, but darkness closed in, and I felt myself drifting into unconsciousness.

"Get her out of here, Mateo," said Nate, turning to leave.

By the time Mateo placed me in a wheelchair and covered me with a blanket, I was utterly powerless to fight him. He guided us toward the service elevator, occasionally passing other passengers who were still up roaming around the deck. I attempted to lock eyes with them, but my lack of focus prevented me from doing so. We boarded the elevator unnoticed and descended to the ship's lower levels.

And that's when my nightmare really began.

CHAPTER ELEVEN

Megan

I was lying on my side, my arms stretched painfully behind my back. The air reeked of oil and bleach, and a relentless pounding hammered in my head.

I tried to open my eyes, but my eyelids were so heavy, it took several minutes to do it. Deciding to tackle one thing at a time, I directed my attention toward my shoulders, where most of my discomfort was. I couldn't seem to move my arms in front of me. As I attempted to pull one arm, my other arm experienced a painful pull in the same direction. My hands were bound behind me. My eyes flew open and my heart pounded wildly at the realization of that thought.

Once my vision adapted to the darkened room, I could see that I was in some type of storeroom. Cleaning supplies were neatly arranged on metal shelves on two walls. That explained the bleach scent. The floor emitted an oil smell, causing me to feel nauseous and struggle to sit upright in order to escape the odor. My shoulders ached, and my head continued to pound in rhythm with my heart. I can't say how long I sat there, leaning against a box, but eventually the fog cleared and my thoughts became clearer. I tried to recall the last thing I remembered. I had dinner with my mom, Rochelle, and Nate.

No, wait. After that, Nate and I left the dining room together. I suddenly felt dizzy and then a crew member attempted to lead me away. I had been alarmed and confused and had cried out to Nate. The memory of his expression and words flooded my mind.

You will do as you are told or you will end up dead.

Everything after that was blank until now. Why would Nate say that to me? And why had he left me in the care of a crew member? Did he actually do that? I couldn't remember anything more, and I was entirely in the dark about what had transpired after I blacked out. It was apparent that I had been tied up and confined in a storage room by someone. But who? Was it Nate or the crew member? And the million-dollar question was, why? I couldn't make sense of any of it.

I scooted across the room, my evening gown twisting beneath me with each movement. Frustrated, I sent my shoes flying into a corner with a kick. After a while, I managed to pull myself up and face away from the door, testing the handle. It was no surprise that it was locked. I yelled for help. I flung myself against the door, trying to get it open or at least attract someone's attention.

I was met with nothing but a persistent humming that resembled some type of engine noise. That didn't help me determine what part of the ship I was in. The noise could be anything coming from anywhere. I crumpled to the ground, sobbing. As I prepared to make another attempt, I heard footsteps approaching.

"Help! I'm in here!"

The doorknob shook with the insertion of a key. A shadowy shape in the doorway entered the room, groping for the light switch on the wall. Light flooded into the room, and I averted my gaze, my eyes sensitive to the brightness. After blinking several times, I looked up and saw Nate. He had traded his tuxedo for shorts and a polo shirt, sunglasses perched on his head. My eyes darted around the room, desperately searching for my clutch. My cell phone was in there, probably with a dead battery, but it was worth a shot. With no sign of it anywhere, I shifted my focus back to Nate.

"Nate! What is going on?" I cried.

He pulled a roll of silver electrical tape from his back pocket and tore a piece off. Without saying a word, he pushed me down by my shoulders then bent down and forcefully slapped the tape across my mouth. I shook my head, and despite my efforts to scream, the tape ensured my voice remained muffled.

Nate crouched down to meet my gaze. His eyes were filled with an icy coldness. I struggled to reconcile this version of him with the man I had spent the last two days with. He was either a world-class actor or a complete psychopath. Fresh tears filled my eyes because it was obvious which one he was. The realization filled me with a terror I had never experienced before. I was shocked at my own stupidity for putting my trust in him. I knew better than to fall for a man I had just met. Things like that only happened in romcoms. Those plots were far from realistic, and yet I had unwittingly played into his hands, just as he had expected me to. Was I actually that pathetic? The moment I asked myself the question, I already had the answer. I wanted to deliver the new Megan a direct punch to the face for being such an idiot. Instead, I blinked vigorously to prevent the waterworks from starting again.

"Megan, I wish things could have been different for us. I truly do. I was honesty starting to like you. But here's the thing. One of my girls met with an unfortunate accident. And seeing as how that product was already sold, I need a replacement or our client will be unhappy. When a client is unhappy, my boss is unhappy. And that's never a good thing. Believe it or not, human traffickers take their responsibility to their buyers quite seriously, Megan. So you see, I really have no choice. You will have to replace Desiree."

Was he freaking serious? He was planning on selling me? I never imagined anything could be worse than my fiancé dumping me for another woman right before our wedding, but this proved me wrong. Being sold into sex slavery far surpassed any trauma Brian had inflicted on me.

I sat there in total disbelief. How could I not know Nate worked for a human trafficking ring? Was I so enamored with him I somehow missed a massive red flag? It was beyond unimaginable. And why me? I wasn't anyone important. I was just an ordinary person with average looks. A kindergarten teacher from Orange County. This wasn't the type of thing that happened to people like me. I didn't understand how he planned to get away with this unnoticed. Then the answer came crashing down on me like a ton of bricks.

Every year, 200 people vanish mysteriously while on cruises.

Of course he could get away with it. I realized I was asking myself the wrong question. I should ask myself what I was going to do to prevent being sold into a trafficking ring. The setup couldn't have been more perfect. We were in Mexico. Did American law enforcement have to wait until the ship returned to Los Angeles to take any action? Would the FBI even be able to help? The crew's involvement would make it almost impossible for anyone to intervene in these people's kidnapping and trafficking plans. When we docked in Playa del Carmen, they could take me off the ship. Or have me quietly slip away unnoticed in the middle of the night. They had gotten me this far without anyone stopping them. And no one would ever find out what happened to me. It was the worst possible thing that could happen to me on the cruise. My most frightening nightmare come true. My eyes must have given away my fear to Nate. I tried to reason with him, shaking my head as I attempted to speak.

"Don't worry, Megan. Your mother will be fine. The cruise line will give her a nice settlement and she will eventually get over your disappearance. People fall overboard more often than you think. Or maybe we'll convince her you got off the ship in Playa del Carmen to go find your ex-fiancé and met with foul play. Whatever. Once she accepts it, closure will come for her."

I was convinced my mother would never believe that I fell overboard in an accident or went in search of Brian. She knew me too well to buy into either of those stories. She would continue to apply pressure on the cruise line until she learned the truth about what happened to me. But if she pushed too hard, I feared it could endanger her life. I knew my mom, and she would never come to terms with my disappearance, nor would she ever get closure. And that could be the very thing that saved me. Or it might cost both of us our lives.

CHAPTER TWELVE

Michelle

I stretched and removed my sleep mask and earplugs. The room was completely devoid of any light, thanks to the blackout curtains. Turning my attention to the bedside clock, I discovered it was already 7:00 a.m. I usually sleep in, but wanted to get an early start on shopping today. Rochelle and I intended to get off the ship when we docked in Playa del Carmen and spend the day wandering the shops until midafternoon. Afterward, I would come back and spend the rest of the afternoon and evening with Megan.

I quickly glanced at Megan's bed and saw it was neatly made. I was asleep immediately after I got in from dinner last night, so I didn't hear Megan come in. My sleep mask and earplugs ensured I wasn't disturbed. Unlike me, my daughter was always an early riser. She must have gotten up and already left for breakfast before heading to the pool.

When Megan's dad was still alive, I would wake up every morning at six o'clock to make him breakfast and prepare his work lunch. I never enjoyed that, as I really wasn't a fan of early mornings. Nevertheless, I did it for my husband and never complained. But it has been years since I last had to wake up that early every day. Now I have the luxury of languishing in bed as long as I please.

I swung my legs over the side of the bed, stretched, and began mentally mapping out my day. I fell in love with Mexico on my last trip here, and couldn't wait to explore it some more. I just hoped Megan would find something to occupy her time and not isolate herself in the room reading. Although that would make me feel better than her spending the day at the pool with Nate as she said she might. I wasn't thrilled with this relative stranger who seemed to have attached himself to her side. I found him too slick for my taste, and my gut told me he wasn't genuine in the image he projected. And I worried she would rebound with the first man who paid attention to her. But I realized that the harder I protested, the more Megan would dig her heels in and stubbornly hold on to him, just to show me I was mistaken. Without a doubt, my daughter was headstrong.

After taking a hot shower and getting dressed, I called Rochelle's room, and we made plans to meet and disembark together. I settled on shorts, a light, button-down shirt, comfy sandals, and a wide-brimmed hat to shield me from the sun. I didn't need any sunlight on my face at my age. I covered my face, arms, and legs with sunblock and grabbed my fanny pack. I knew fanny packs were considered terribly unfashionable, but I wasn't willing to risk having my shoulder bag stolen while walking around Playa del Carmen, especially while I was distracted shopping.

I met Rochelle at the breakfast buffet and hastily scanned the area, hoping to spot Megan. Not seeing her anywhere, I made a mental note to swing by the pool before we left to touch base with her. We quickly finished breakfast and exited the dining room as the announcement that we had docked in Playa del Carmen played over the ship's speakers.

"Michelle, we need to get going before the line to get off the ship gets any longer," prompted Rochelle, tugging my arm toward her and away from the pool.

"This will only take a second. Come on," I urged, yanking my arm out of her grasp.

Rochelle followed me begrudgingly, rolling her eyes as she did so.

We were close to the pool and arrived within minutes. With one hand holding my hat and the other shielding my eyes, I stood on the deck under the early morning sun.

"I don't see her," I said.

"We probably just missed her at breakfast. She might have gone back to change into her suit. She's fine, Michelle. We'll catch up with her when we get back."

Frowning, I took another quick look around the pool area. Rochelle was right. Megan was an adult. She was fine.

"Okay. Let's go," I murmured, following Rochelle off the pool deck.

Waiting in line to get off the ship, I couldn't shake the nagging worry of not seeing Megan. I again told myself I was being ridiculous, and by the time we set foot on land, I was, at most, mildly annoyed that I had missed her.

We strolled through the shops in Playa del Carmen's tourist area for hours, and by the time we were ready for lunch, I had several full bags in tow. We enjoyed tacos and margaritas on the patio of a small café, where a cool breeze and my drink combined to create a soothing sensation. But my mind kept going back to Megan, hoping she was having a good time.

"Hey. Where are you?" asked Rochelle. "You look like you're a million miles away."

"Just thinking about Megan. I know she's hurting over Brian. And the fact that he's getting married this weekend and so close to here . . . well, it just feels like an excessively cruel coincidence."

"I agree, it does. The new guy seems to be a nice distraction for her though. But I worry she might try to see Brian while she's here in a last-ditch attempt to save their relationship."

The sip of margarita I had just swallowed went down wrong, causing me to cough. "What? Why would you say that? She wouldn't try to see Brian."

"I don't know. I'm just saying when people are hurt, they do unexpected things, that's all."

"Where did you get that? Dr. Ruth? That's ridiculous, Rochelle. I know she's hurting, but Megan would never contact Brian before his wedding to try to patch things up. And if she ever *did* think about doing that, she would insist that we go with her. Traipsing around Mexico alone is so not her style."

"I don't know, Michelle. Maybe you don't give Megan enough credit. She might surprise you," Rochelle replied, shrugging dismissively as she resumed sipping her margarita.

But I couldn't shake my sense of unease. There was no way Megan would do that. *Would she?*

I pushed the thought out of my mind. I knew my daughter. Even though she may be hurt and angry, she would never humiliate herself by groveling for a second chance with Brian. She deserved better than that little pissant. Besides, she didn't even want to get off the ship with me and Rochelle. She would never disembark alone.

Satisfied that Megan was safely relaxing poolside on the ship, I finished my drink and we resumed shopping. It wasn't until later that evening that my mother's intuition let me know that something was absolutely wrong.

CHAPTER THIRTEEN

Megan

Crying caused my nose to become congested, and the tape prevented me from breathing through my mouth. I was teetering on the edge of a panic attack, still reeling from Nate's confession. I pressed against the wall, forcing myself to calm down. Crying wouldn't free me from the storage room I was trapped in.

I concentrated on slow breaths through my nose until my heartbeat slowed to a somewhat normal pace. I had to free my hands. I was clear about that much. Without that, I would be absolutely helpless to defend myself. I crouched on the floor and exerted all my strength to stand up and flip on the light switch. A quick survey of the room revealed no potential tools to cut the zip ties holding my hands together. I searched through the shelving, pushing aside containers of cleaning supplies with my head, hoping to find something useful. The shelves were stocked with plastic containers of bleach and other cleaning agents alongside dust rags and sponges. Nothing that would be useful.

I dropped to the floor again and that's when I saw it. There was a glass bottle lying on its side behind the bottom shelf. I scrambled to my knees and struggled to move the shelf using my head, but it proved impossible. Despite my limited finger mobility, I managed to turn around and slide the metal shelving a few inches apart. I nudged the bottle forward by sliding my foot behind it. With a final push, it rolled out toward me, and I shimmied around until I could grab it. I was in an awkward position that strained my shoulders. But I didn't care. The only thing that mattered to me in that moment was the glass bottle I had. I scooted to the far end of the room, facing the door, while still holding the bottle. There were boxes there I could hide the bottle between in case someone entered. Sweat beaded on my forehead and my fingers were slippery from the effort, but I maintained a tight grip. I knew I just had one chance at getting this right. I had to break the top part of the bottle, leaving the bottom untouched to cut my bindings. It would be too difficult to hold a piece of glass and try to saw though the zip ties. My fingertips didn't have enough range of motion to reach them. Whoever bound my hands knew what they were doing. My ability to move was severely restricted.

It required several attempts before I was able to grasp the bottom of the bottle and break the top off. It took what felt like hours, but I finally did it. I pushed the broken glass shards behind the boxes using my feet. Then I made my way to the light switch and, using my head, pushed it to the off position. I didn't want anyone to know I had been snooping around. Best to give them the impression that I was helpless and being cooperative.

Once I was back in position, I worked the zip tie across the bottle's jagged top. Perfecting the technique was difficult and progress was slow. I had to be careful to not accidentally cut myself. It would take hours to cut through the zip ties at this pace. But I had no other choice. I could sit there and wait to be taken by a deranged psychopath who thought it was acceptable to sell a woman, or fight my way out and escape. There was no question. It was a no-brainer.

I don't know how long I worked on cutting my ties, but I could tell I was making some progress. I struggled to touch the edge of the restraint with my fingertips, but I discovered a small tear in the plastic. It was working, and that gave me a renewed sense of hope. I kept at it, only resting briefly when my hands cramped. I wasn't sure what I would do if someone checked my binding. I would just have to make sure they didn't.

It was during one of my rest periods that I heard footsteps approaching again. I hastily shoved the bottle between the boxes and settled onto my side, forcing myself to become teary-eyed. Shedding tears wasn't challenging. I was genuinely petrified. I realized that I had to give an Oscar-worthy performance to trick my captors into believing they held the upper hand and were still in control. I had to convince them I had no intention of trying to get away. There was no doubt that if they thought for one second I was planning something or even thinking about running, they would ensure I never escaped.

The door opened and light flooded the room. I blinked and raised my head, expecting to see Nate. Instead, a stranger stared down at me. With one hand, he gripped a bottle of water, while the other held zip ties. He set the water down, pulled out a pocketknife, and headed in my direction. My heart beat faster. I was convinced he planned to cut my ties briefly so I could have a drink and then tie me up again. I couldn't allow that to happen. The cut in my restraints would definitely catch his attention, and then I would be finished. My mind raced as I thought about waiting for him to untie me and then using the broken bottle to stab him in the neck. But could I get to the bottle in time? Not likely. And even if I could, would he intervene before I could use the weapon against him? Almost certainly. He had a clear physical advantage over me. I decided to go with Plan B and swiftly positioned myself against the shelf, grasping the metal leg firmly. Within seconds he reached me and forcefully ripped the tape from my mouth, causing me to let out a painful cry.

Then I let loose a blood-curdling scream at the very top of my lungs.

Startled by my outburst, the man was taken aback as the sound reverberated off the walls of the small storage room. He stopped suddenly, mouth hanging open for a few seconds, before he snapped out of it.

"Hey, shut up!"

"No! Don't hurt me! Help!" I continued to scream.

"For fuck's sake. Stop screaming. No one can hear you, anyway."

I didn't allow that to deter me. If no one could hear me, then he wouldn't care if I screeched until I passed out. I screamed even louder and desperately gripped the rack leg, prepared for him to wrench me loose forcefully.

"What the hell, lady!"

He bent down and removed the lid from the water bottle. "Do you want a fucking drink of water or not?"

I stopped screaming when he held the bottle up to my face. I titled my head forward as he poured the contents of the bottle into my mouth. As I gulped down the water, I never took my eyes off him. I wiped the excess water from my chin on my shoulder, still holding his gaze.

He put the cap back on the water and sat the bottle down next to me before he stood up and turned to the door.

"Crazy fucking bitch," he mumbled as he turned off the light and let the door click shut behind him.

I smiled to myself. Then I fished the bottle out from between the boxes behind me and resumed working on my restraints. That didn't last long, however. Whatever drug was in the water took effect in a hurry, and my eyes refused to stay open. My movements were sluggish and slow, and my thoughts were disjointed. I knew I couldn't risk working on the zip ties in that condition, so I pushed the broken bottle toward the stack of boxes and yielded to the drowsiness. My last thought, while lying in the dark on the cold floor, was that I couldn't trust these people not to drug me again.

I prayed it wasn't too late and this wasn't the end for me.

CHAPTER FOURTEEN

Michelle

I slowly made my way up the walkway to the ship, feeling as if my feet were encased in cement. Even though it was late afternoon, the Mexico sun scorched my bare shoulders with a relentless intensity. All I wanted to do was take a refreshing shower and spend the evening with my daughter. I hadn't expected to be back this late, but Rochelle kept finding reasons to stay in Playa del Carmen. More than once, she insisted on visiting *just one more shop*. Despite my late arrival back on the ship, I could at least still have dinner with Megan and maybe catch a show or try our luck at one of the casinos.

I hadn't had nearly enough time with my daughter on the trip, and we only had a few days left. She had been spending all of her time with Nate. Although I was glad she was enjoying herself and not staying in the cabin reading, I felt somewhat disappointed that we hadn't done more together. I saw this cruise as the perfect chance for some mother-daughter bonding. Now, more than ever, she needed me after losing Brian.

"Wanna grab dinner in a couple of hours?" asked Rochelle.

"Oh, I don't know. I was hoping to spend some time with Megan tonight. I feel like I haven't seen much of her since we've been here. Would you mind if I beg off for tonight? We can do something tomorrow."

"Of course. You go do something fun with Megan and I'll find something to do. I have my eye on a couple of bachelors I saw at the shuffleboard deck yesterday," she said, laughing.

"Of course you do," I responded, playfully rolling my eyes at her.

Rochelle always had a never-ending line of suitors waiting in the wings. I wasn't sure how she did it, but that wasn't my style. After Megan's dad passed, I just never had the desire to try to meet anyone else. He was the love of my life, and no one else would ever measure up to him.

Rochelle and I each headed for our rooms, promising to connect in the morning. I inserted my room card into the door lock, fully expecting to find Megan inside reading, waiting for my return. But the room, bathroom, and balcony were all empty. I quickly scanned the small area, but everything appeared undisturbed, exactly as I had left it that morning. I thought that was strange since I was sure Megan would have returned to the room at some point during the day. But it wasn't entirely impossible. If she met up with Nate, as I was certain she had, they might still be at the pool and had just lost track of time.

I opted for a quick shower and clothing change so Megan could have the bathroom when she returned. After my shower, I tried flipping through channels for a movie, but couldn't focus. It annoyed me that Megan hadn't bothered to call the room or even leave me a message to inform me of her plans. I tried to call her cell, but it went directly to voicemail. That didn't come as a surprise. I didn't know if she had international calling or packed her phone charger. When I thought about it, I wasn't even sure she had her cell phone with her on the trip.

I was getting restless, so I left a hastily scribbled note on her neatly made bed before I left for the pool to see if she was there.

Went to the pool to find you. Get ready for dinner and wait for me here!

Love, Mom

I grabbed my cruise card and stuffed it into my pants pocket, then hurried down the corridor. I reassured myself that I was overreacting, but because I hadn't seen Megan since last night, I was uneasy. Megan was my only child, and I admit I'd been a bit overly protective of her for most of her life. But I couldn't help it. She was my entire world. I kept reminding myself that she was no longer my little girl, but a grown woman. But despite my efforts to dispel my fears, I couldn't shake my increasing anxiety.

I reached the pool deck and navigated among the tables and sunbathers, stopping briefly to scan the people in the pool in search of my daughter. I turned around and retraced my steps. She was nowhere to be seen. The sound of loud laughter from the bar grabbed my attention, and I spun around to see Nate on a bar stool, laughing with the bartender. Relief washed over me. I smiled as I moved through the crowd toward him.

"Nate, hello!" I exclaimed, as I waved to him.

He looked up and smiled. "Hello, Michelle. How was your shopping trip?"

"Uh, fine, thanks. Where is Megan?"

"I don't have a clue, actually."

My stomach did a flip.

"What do you mean?"

"I haven't seen her all day. I had hoped she would be here this morning, but she wasn't."

"Have you been here all day?" I questioned, my voice rising.

"Off and on, hoping to run into Megan."

"Well, when did you last see her? Did you two have plans to meet today?"

"I last saw her after drinks last night when we left the bar. She was pretty tipsy by the time we left for our rooms. We made plans to meet here this morning, but as I mentioned, she didn't show up."

"Well, did you go to our room to check on her?" I asked, feeling my panic grow.

"No, Michelle, I didn't. I thought maybe she was embarrassed about drinking so much last night, and maybe she didn't remember making plans with me. Or maybe she changed her mind and decided to go shopping with you and your friend, after all."

"Drunk? Megan? That's not like her at all. And she didn't go shopping with us, Nate. She wasn't in the room when I got up this morning. I thought she had gotten up early and already left, but now I'm not so sure she ever came back to the room last night at all. I . . . I think I need to call security," I stammered, glancing around and nervously twisting my hands.

Standing up, Nate gently touched my shoulder. "Hang on, Michelle. She has to be here somewhere. She probably just wanted to spend some time alone. Last night she mentioned wanting to catch up on some reading. I'll bet she's tucked away in a quiet corner with a book and has just lost track of the time. I'll help you find her. Just stay calm. I'm sure she's fine."

"Okay. You're probably right," I responded, grateful for his reassurance and willingness to help.

He placed a few bills on the bar as a tip, nodding his thanks to the bartender, and extended his arm to me. I threaded my arm through his, appreciating the support, but my stomach still churned with worry as he led me away from the pool deck to the main atrium.

"Let's start with the dining room and work our way through the gift shops and the casinos."

I nodded in agreement, content to be guided by someone else in control.

Nate's organized search of the ship had us looking for Megan for the next several hours in any place we believed she could have gone. By that time, dinner was being served and guests were filing into the various dining rooms.

"I'm worried, Nate. We should have seen her by now," I said.

"It's a big ship, Michelle. I'll bet she's back in the room by now," he suggested.

"You're right. She must be. I completely forgot that I left her a note to stay there. She's probably worried about *me* now, wondering why I'm not back yet. I'm sorry to have wasted your time, Nate."

"It's no trouble. I'm here for as long as it takes to find her. But I'm sure she's probably back in the room by now," he said.

Nate stayed by my side as we moved toward the escalator leading to the upper deck and my room. When we arrived at the door, my hand trembled as I inserted the card into the lock. The door lock clicked, and it felt like an eternity before I could push it open.

"Megan?" I called out, stepping inside.

But the room was empty. Untouched since I was last there, with the note I left for Megan still on her bed.

I started breathing rapidly, overwhelmed by panic. Something terrible had happened to my daughter. I could *feel* it. I could sense it throughout every cell in my body.

"I'm going to call Rochelle. And security," I stated, brushing past Nate and heading toward the bedside phone.

I called Rochelle's room before anyone else. "Megan's missing. I'm calling security. I'm really scared, Rochelle. Can you come to my room?"

Rochelle agreed to come over immediately. Ending the call hastily, I dialed security on the speed dial. With a tight grip on the receiver, I eagerly waited for someone to answer the call, while I tried, but failed, to convince myself Megan was safe.

CHAPTER FIFTEEN

Megan

My hands were nearly freed. My shoulders throbbed from the exertion of the repetitive motion and from being stretched behind me for so long. I used the glass to tear the last bit of the plastic zip ties and then relaxed, allowing my arms to return to a more comfortable position. The relief was immediate, and I rolled my shoulders to relieve the stiffness.

I had no clue when someone might be back again, so I only allowed myself a moment of rest. There weren't many options for me after thinking about a plan and considering the limited stockpile in the storeroom. The one thing I had to defend myself with was the broken bottle. If that man returned, or someone of similar build, I couldn't defeat him with merely a broken bottle. He was twice my size. I had no chance of winning a fight against him. I needed to catch him off guard and temporarily disable him so I could escape.

I walked to the far wall and turned on the light switch, blinking as my eyes adjusted to the sudden brightness. Then I quickly poured out the contents of a spray bottle onto the floor in the room's corner. Next, I grabbed a bottle of bleach from one of the shelves and filled the plastic bottle. The overpowering scent left a burning sensation in my nostrils. I realized my plan wasn't foolproof, and I would get one chance to get it right. But I had to give it a shot. I couldn't just sit idly by and wait for those people to remove me from the ship. I was smart enough to understand that if that occurred, my chances of escape would plummet to nearly zero. I had to escape now or I probably wouldn't survive.

I moved to the stack of boxes and began peeling the clear packing tape from them. Assuming I lived long enough, I figured I could use it to tie him up. If I wrapped his hands and feet tightly with enough tape, it would take him a while to free himself, even if it didn't have the stickiness or strength of duct tape. Once I had enough tape from a few boxes, I moved to the opposite wall. With one hand holding the broken bottle and the other gripping the spray bottle filled with bleach, I turned off the light and sank to the floor to wait. I positioned myself behind the door, out of sight, in order to lure anyone who entered the room to search for me. Like I said, not a foolproof plan—not by a long shot. But it was the best I could come up with. My idea was to douse his face with bleach and then attack him with the broken bottle. Then I would restrain him.

That's how I pictured things would go, at least.

But the thought of thrusting that sharp glass into another person sickened me. I was relying on the bleach to immobilize him long enough so I could secure him and escape. With any luck, he would have zip ties with him again. If not, I'd be left with no choice but to use the packing tape and hope for the best.

Quietly positioned behind the door, I remained alert, listening for the sound of approaching footsteps. My mouth was parched and my stomach growled. But I didn't dare drink any of the water left in the bottle given to me by the man. I focused on my game plan to distract myself from the burning thirst. I rehearsed my moves multiple times so I would be prepared when the door opened.

The sound of footsteps took what felt like hours to reach me, but I had lost all track of time since being taken. I stood up quietly, ready to strike. But the footsteps grew more distant. It turned out to be a false alarm. I banged on the door with all my might. Was there someone out there who could help me? I yelled and pounded on the door until I was certain they were gone. There was no chance they didn't hear me. That information implied I was in a restricted area of the ship, accessible only to those who were involved in my abduction. I crumpled to the ground, water pooling in my eyes. It was hard not to be discouraged. Even if I were to escape the room I was trapped in, would I be able to find my way to safety on the upper decks? Taking that risk was a massive gamble. Yet one I had to take in order to have any chance of escape.

It didn't take long for me to hear more footsteps coming. I stood up rapidly, holding the spray bottle at arm's length, prepared to defend against anyone entering the room. My heart sped up at the sound of the jingling door handle.

This was what it all came down to. This was the moment of truth. I was taking rapid breaths, anxious because I knew everything hinged on getting the timing right. If I acted too soon, I would risk exposing my position and losing the element of surprise. Waiting too long would likely result in the man confiscating my makeshift weapons. I didn't even want to think about the consequences if that happened.

Time seemed to slow down as the door swung open and light leaked in from the hallway. In order to minimize the impact of the overhead lighting on my vision, I turned toward the light and allowed my eyes to adjust as much as possible before the tiny storeroom was bathed in brightness.

I heard him advancing further into the room and a second later the lights flickered on. I blinked rapidly and waited for him to come all the way in. After a moment of hesitation, he stepped in and let the door swing shut behind him. He saw me in his peripheral vision, and made a grab for me, but he wasn't fast enough. I had the element of surprise and pumped the spray bottle at his face repeatedly. In a blind rage, his arms flailed in front of him, desperately trying to find me, but his hands closed around empty space. I directed the spray toward his open mouth and eyes. I needed him to be quiet. After a few seconds, he began to make a horrible, strangled choking noise. He clutched at his throat and attempted to wipe his eyes, only forcing more bleach into them. Gasping for air, he was now in a complete state of panic. Using the long handle of a mop, I pushed him against the wall and then used it to strike him on the head. His hands remained on his face as he slid to the floor. Seizing the chance, I swiftly bound his wrists together while they were close to his face.

Once that was done, he struggled intensely. I wound strips of tape tightly around his eyes and over his mouth to muffle his cries. He was so focused on removing the tape from his face that he stopped trying to kick me. I took advantage of his temporary confusion to bind his ankles and used the remaining tape to fasten his hands and feet to the closest shelf leg.

Satisfied I had done all I could, I searched him for a cell phone, keys, or any kind of weapon. All I uncovered was an old receipt and a handful of coins. He kicked and struggled, his muffled screams persisting the whole time. I watched as he desperately continued to try to remove the tape from his eyes and mouth, questioning if I had taken things too far and caused him serious harm. I had no clue about the damage bleach could cause to eyes or soft tissue. When I made my plan, it seemed like a good way to disable him. Still, I questioned my decision as I watched him frantically trying to remove the tape. He was in full panic mode, a complete departure from the tough criminal facade he had assumed earlier. I knew for certain that he would escape his restraints at some point, and I had no intention of being nearby when that happened.

I told myself he would kill me the first chance he got, so I couldn't have any sympathy for him or anyone else connected to my abduction. I cast one final glance at him before turning off the lights, then I gingerly cracked open the door and peeked my head out. Scanning the corridor, I saw it was empty. Seeing that was enough for me. Catching sight of my strappy heels in the corner, I decided that I would be faster without them and chose to go barefoot. I hiked up my evening gown, making it easier to move, then tugged the door open wider and cautiously stepped into the hallway. After checking both directions, I turned right and took off like a bat out of hell.

CHAPTER SIXTEEN

Michelle

While I waited with Nate for security, I paced around the room nervously. A knock on the door jolted me out of my thoughts, prompting Nate to move toward the small vestibule. I stopped and eagerly awaited as he opened the door. My shoulders relaxed when I saw it was Rochelle.

What was taking security so long to get here?

Rochelle came directly toward me, grasped my hand, and guided me to the couch.

"Michelle, don't you think you're blowing things out of proportion just a little? Megan is a grown woman. She's probably just hooked up with some new friends and is out having some fun."

She glanced in Nate's direction, but he abruptly averted his gaze. I wondered if he shared Rochelle's perception that I was exaggerating the situation.

"No, I don't think I'm overreacting, and I can't believe you would say that to me. You know Megan, Rochelle. Something is wrong. You have to know that, right?" I implored, pulling my hand away from hers.

I expected Rochelle to provide some support, not to criticize me for being overprotective of my adult daughter. Truthfully, I was more than a little irritated with her because of it. Before I could react further, another knock on the door made me spring up and open it.

When I swung the door open, I was greeted by a tall man in uniform, holding a walkie talkie and smiling at me.

"Hello, I'm Captain Antonio Perez, Head of Security for the *Jewel of the Sea.* May I come in?"

"Yes, of course. Forgive my lack of manners, Captain Perez. I'm just so worried about my daughter I'm not thinking clearly."

I stepped out of the way and gestured for him to come into the room, motioning toward the couch. Rochelle got up and moved to sit on the end of my bed, facing the couch, while Nate took the chair. I sat down beside Captain Perez and folded my hands in my lap, taking a deep, calming breath.

"So, Ms. Hamilton. Why don't you tell me what the problem is?"

"I haven't seen my daughter Megan since last night at dinner. When I woke up this morning, she wasn't in the room. I assumed she was already up and about, so I went into Playa del Carmen for the day with my friend Rochelle," I said, motioning toward Rochelle.

"And you haven't heard from her this evening?"

"No. She was supposed to meet her friend Nate here at the pool this morning, but never showed up."

Nate nodded in agreement as Captain Perez glanced over at him.

"Ms. Hamilton, your daughter is an adult, correct?"

I nodded, tension taking hold of me as I realized where the conversation was headed.

"I'm sure she is fine. She most likely got off the ship today to go into Playa del Carmen and is still out having a wonderful time sightseeing. We don't leave for Los Angeles for a few days, and I'm sure she'll turn up before then. These situations almost always turn out to be a misunderstanding."

His pitiful gaze made me bristle, and it infuriated me he wasn't taking Megan's disappearance more seriously.

"No, you're wrong. There is no way Megan got off the ship alone to go into Mexico. Absolutely no way. Tell him, Rochelle," I prompted, turning to face my best friend.

"Michelle, maybe Megan is getting braver. I hate to say it, but maybe she went to look for Brian's wedding. Costa Maya is very close. She could have easily gotten off the ship and taken a taxi there."

Rochelle's words felt like a slap in the face. How could she say something like that?

"What? She would never do that. I told you before, and I'm telling you again, Megan would never get off this ship alone, and certainly not to go find Brian's wedding! Why am I the only one taking this seriously?"

I stood up and shifted my gaze from Rochelle to Perez then to Nate. They undoubtedly thought I was in denial. I was aware that I sounded somewhat out of control, perhaps even a bit manic. But it was close to how I was feeling. I was convinced Megan was on the ship, and I intended to find her. Even if I had to do it on my own.

"Brian is her ex-fiancé who just called off their wedding a few weeks ago. He is marrying someone else in Costa Maya this weekend," said Rochelle, directing the statement to Captain Perez.

I clenched my fists at my sides and shot Rochelle a furious glance.

"Michelle, I'm sorry. I know you don't want to hear this. But I think you're making something out of nothing here. I realize Megan is your only child and you two are close, but you've always been so overprotective of her. She is a grown woman, and can take off for the day if she wants to."

I looked at Nate for support, but he avoided eye contact, clearly unwilling to defend me.

"Okay, let's just calm down. I will have my staff check for activity on her sea card, and if that doesn't show her leaving the ship today, then will do a quick search on board for your daughter," said Captain Perez. "We can also make a general announcement for her to call a courtesy phone. I'm sure we will either find her having a wonderful time on the ship or confirm she disembarked sometime today to go into Playa del Carmen."

I slumped onto the couch, overwhelmed and defeated, as the weight of worry settled heavily on my shoulders like a cement block.

"When will that happen?" I asked him.

"Immediately. I will assign a few of my night staff to the task and should have some answers for you by morning. Of course, if your daughter comes back to the room tonight, please call me right away."

"Yes, of course I will. I'm going to make another round of the ship myself," I replied.

"Ms. Hamilton, it might be best if you stay in the room, in case Megan comes back here."

"I can't just sit here and do nothing, Captain Perez. My daughter is out there somewhere, and I know she needs my help."

"Rochelle and I can keep looking," suggested Nate.

Rochelle nodded, but my anger towards her prevented any acknowledgement from me.

"If we find anything, I will call you right away," promised Nate.

"Thank you, Nate."

"In the meantime, I would ask you to look through your daughter's things and see if you can tell if anything is missing. Clothing, toiletries, medications. Things she might need for a day trip," said Captain Perez.

"I'll do that," I answered as I walked to the door.

Captain Perez followed my lead and stood up to shake my hand. "I know this is easier said than done, but try not to worry, Ms. Hamilton. Our ship is exceedingly safe, and if she is here, we will find her."

If she was here? I understood his meaning, although I didn't comment. He believed Megan had gotten off the ship earlier today. I knew he was wrong.

Rochelle and Nate left the room with the head of security, leaving me alone with my thoughts. It couldn't believe the unexpected direction my trip had taken. Megan was gone, and no one seemed very concerned about my missing daughter except for me.

I sank onto the couch, letting my head fall back on the cushions. *Where are you Megan?*

CHAPTER SEVENTEEN

Megan

I attempted to be as silent as I could when I initially left the storeroom. I was uncertain if there was anyone in the area who might harm me or try to capture me again. And of course, there was always the looming threat of Nate's return. Despite this, after ten minutes of getting lost in the labyrinth of hallways without seeing another person, I felt safe enough to run, my only objective being to reach help.

I passed occasional doors which were all locked. The corridors appeared identical, and I suspected I was going in circles. The absence of labels on the doors made it impossible for me to know if I had gone that way before. I was lost and wasn't sure how to reach the public decks without knowing my location. I needed to devise a plan, but had no way to do that.

I rounded a corner at top speed, narrowly missing crashing into a crew member, where I skidded to a stop, gasping for air. I saw the shock in his eyes as he took a step back. Not knowing if any other staff were involved in the operation other than the crew member who helped Nate abduct me, I had no option but to trust him. If I kept silent and took off running, he would surely alert someone, and I couldn't afford to take that risk. Now that he had seen me, I had to ask for help. And even though I knew at least one crew member had been instrumental in my abduction, that didn't necessarily implicate *this* crew member.

I struggled to catch my breath as the words tumbled out of me. "Help me!" I couldn't hold back the tears as I sobbed. "There's a man, and he's going to come after me. He had me tied up in a room. He's trying to kidnap me!"

"Whoa, calm down, miss," he urged, gripping my shoulders while he tried to steady me.

I shook my head in response. "No! I need you to call security, please! He could find me any minute!"

"Okay, I understand. Just give me a minute. I'm calling right now. See?" he said.

As he showed me his radio, his nervousness was clear, and my appearance and hysteria surely didn't help. I had been held captive in a dark room with no access to food and very little spiked water for . . . *how long?* I didn't know, exactly. But I was certain I appeared disheveled at best.

As the man stepped away, I slid down the wall and settled on my haunches. I continued searching the corridor, worried that Nate or someone else would appear and take me back to the small storeroom, waiting to be taken off the ship. The man's voice was low as he spoke on his radio, and I watched him, trying to hear the conversation. I couldn't decipher his words, but I heard someone replying to him. However, it was filled with static and too hard to understand. He looked back at me after a moment.

"I've alerted the head of security and he will meet us on an upper deck. It's just a short walk. Can you make it?" he asked, offering his hand to help me up.

"Yes, thank you," I replied, reaching for his hand.

He silently guided me through multiple hallways, looking back occasionally to be sure I was still following him. I remained skeptical of him, so I stayed on guard and continued to search for any signs of my captors. With each new hallway we encountered, my heart quickened. Yet every time the coast was clear, my comfort level increased. By now, I knew my mom must be extremely worried. Given her age, I was worried about her health, and stress like this could easily have a negative effect on her. My mom continued to occupy my thoughts, but I was almost certain I had eluded my captors, so I was calming down. But as we rounded a corner, the sight that greeted me caused me to freeze in place.

Nate appeared relaxed as he casually leaned against the wall, scrolling through his cell phone. I felt my heart drop into my stomach. His eyes met mine, and he flashed me a smile. I was suddenly hit with a wave of sickness. This man was undeniably a psychopath.

"Megan. There you are. I was afraid I'd lost you. Thank you, Mateo. I'll take it from here," he announced, pushing off the wall and starting toward me.

I was only one step away when Mateo grabbed me and forcefully pinned me against the wall.

"No," I cried instinctively, yet knowing it was no use.

Nate's smile immediately faded as he approached me. The moment he took out flex ties from his back pocket, I knew it was over for me and my fate was sealed. They would never let me slip through their grasp again.

"Come on, Megan. Don't fight it. Your buyer will be here tomorrow, and I expect you to be compliant and in good shape by then."

I struggled against him with all my strength, but it was pointless. He overpowered me quickly with Mateo's help.

With my hands secured, Nate roughly steered me along the hallway. I felt utterly hopeless and completely alone. I should have run after I escaped until I reached an upper deck, where I knew I could find help. I wished I'd never stopped when I saw Mateo. I should have recognized him as the person Nate used to help subdue me on deck. But the memory of my capture was still hazy, and I couldn't remember what his face looked like. Trusting him was a stupid move. One I would pay for now.

Dread overtook me as I envisioned my future, and I found myself wishing for a quick death, aware that the alternative would be much worse.

It didn't take long to reach our destination, and Nate unlocked the door to reveal an empty room. There was nothing in it but a bucket tucked away in the far corner of the room. They were without doubt not willing to take any chances with me this time. There was nothing I could defend myself with. Nate's push propelled me into the room, causing me to stumble and fall, unable to steady myself with my hands bound. I felt my head collide with the floor and black spots danced in my vision.

"You should have just left well enough alone, Megan. If you try anything like that again, I'll kill your mother. Do we understand each other?"

A sob escaped me.

He moved in and leaned down. "I asked you a question. Do you understand?"

I nodded in response, too overwhelmed with fear to answer.

"Good," he said, rising. He walked to the bucket and pulled out a bottle of water. He twisted the cap off and positioned himself directly above me. "Sit up. You're going to drink this. All of it."

I didn't react fast enough, and Nate jerked my shoulder while pulling me up by my elbow. I cried out, and he delivered a powerful slap to the side of my face.

"I have had enough of you, Megan. Personally, I think you are way too much trouble for the effort. But for some reason, my boss insists that you're going with the rest of the group to the buyers. So until tomorrow, when we take you into Mexico, you will behave yourself or you'll get your mother killed."

With a powerful yank of my hair, he tilted my head back and poured the water into my mouth. After forcing me to swallow most of the water, he carelessly tossed the bottle aside and released me.

He closed the door and turned off the light without saying another word. I remained on the floor, too overwhelmed to do anything else. At that point, I had no option but to comply. I wouldn't jeopardize my mother's life under any circumstances. I sobbed until the drugs in the water kicked in, unconcerned about my own safety as they took control and I drifted into unconsciousness.

CHAPTER EIGHTEEN

Michelle

Obviously, sleep was out of the question with my daughter missing. I had to be there if she came back to the room. What if she returned and I missed her? Deep down, I knew that wasn't likely to happen. Megan would never allow me to worry like this. Since she hadn't reached out to me, Rochelle, or Nate, she had to know I would be consumed with worry by now. Nate promised he and Rochelle would keep searching the ship for her, but no one would be as thorough as me. The security captain's reaction was lukewarm, and Nate and Rochelle appeared somewhat unconcerned about Megan's disappearance. And I was still surprised by Rochelle's suggestion that Megan might have gone after Brian. That was absurd. Megan hadn't even mentioned Brian at all since arriving on the cruise. She was enjoying her time with Nate and moving on.

Wasn't she?

Worry washed over me as I looked around the empty cabin. Where could she be? The *Jewel of the Sea* was a large ship and still had areas left unsearched by Nate and me. She had to be on the ship somewhere. I tried to rationalize why she hadn't returned to the cabin by now. I paced the small room, my brain struggling to come up with ideas, while my imagination ran wild, envisioning all sorts of terrible scenarios. I forced myself to calm down and approach the situation logically. I could do this. I could find my daughter. I'd done so many other things I never thought I could. I buried my husband and delivered the heartbreaking message to my young daughter that her dad was never coming home. I single-handedly raised Megan without help from anyone. I had a successful career with no experience to back me up. However, this was unlike anything I had ever come up against before. The pain of uncertainty, not knowing Megan's whereabouts or what happened to her, was unbearable. It was torturous.

I tried to convince myself that we had just missed each other coming and going from the stateroom. Since I had been gone most of the day, Megan probably got caught up doing something and lost track of time. I realized I had been in the cabin for no more than a total of about two hours since early this morning. I repeated that in my head countless times. I had to do it to keep myself from spiraling out of control. Sometime after midnight, I settled into the chair to wait for Megan to get in.

I must have drifted off to sleep because when I woke up, sunlight was streaming through the open blinds of the deck's sliding door. I jolted awake and directed my attention to Megan's bed.

Empty. Exactly how it was yesterday morning. Nothing had changed, and no one had slept in it. The sheets were neatly tucked into the mattress, with the pillows undisturbed. Panic immediately took hold. I could no longer fool myself into believing there was a reason for Megan's absence. Something was terribly wrong. I called the security number, but Captain Perez wasn't in his office, so I hurriedly changed my clothes, planning to go find him. Now he would have no choice but to listen to me.

While I ran a brush through my hair, I heard a knock on the door. Hoping maybe it was Megan who lost her sea card, I rushed to unlock it. When I swung the door open, Rochelle and Captain Perez were standing there. I stepped back, my eyes filling with tears that I couldn't control.

They stepped into the cabin and found seats on the couch, while I made my way back to the chair I had slept in the night prior.

"Megan didn't come back last night, Captain Perez. Please, you have to believe me now that something is seriously wrong here," I begged.

"Ms. Hamilton, it doesn't appear that your daughter is on the ship. We have done a cursory search, top to bottom, and were unable to locate her. We made several announcements for her to pick up a courtesy phone, but received no response to those requests. Her sea card was not registered as leaving the ship, and although the cruise line likes to think it unlikely, it's not impossible for a passenger to bypass the staff sometimes in the rush of people exiting the ship. Yesterday was an excessively busy day for the crew, as it was our first day in Playa del Carmen. I have one of my officers reviewing yesterday's security camera footage this morning. If she disembarked the ship when we docked, we might be able to find video footage of it. We do have videotape of her leaving the dining room with Nate right after 2:00 a.m. just as he said they had, but after that, there was no sign of her."

"What do you mean there was no sign of her? Didn't Nate walk her back to our room?"

"They actually went their separate ways after having drinks at the dining room bar, as he stated. He went to his cabin while Megan said she was heading here to your cabin. I confirmed via Nate's sea card that he arrived at his cabin twelve minutes after the shot of them leaving the bar. We don't have any record of Megan using her card for your cabin. It appears her plans changed."

"What? That's impossible. I'm certain Nate told me he walked her to our cabin. Where else would she go? Don't you have video to track her movements after she left Nate?"

"Ms. Hamilton, this ship has approximately 90,000 square feet of interior space. It is virtually impossible for us to have cameras everywhere. They are posted in the most frequented public areas only. The exits were accessible for disembarkation into Mexico at nine o'clock yesterday morning, and passengers started to line up a couple of hours prior to that. It's possible that she fell asleep on a deck chair for a few hours and headed straight for the nearest exit early that morning. We are currently in the process of reviewing the tapes, as I mentioned earlier."

"In her evening gown? That's crazy! She wouldn't do that," I insisted.

"Michelle, according to Nate, Megan had a lot to drink that night. She was drunk when they said goodnight. Maybe she started thinking about Brian and decided to track him down," said Rochelle.

"Rochelle, that you would even suggest that again is unbelievable! You know her better than that," I scoffed, glaring at her.

"Ms. Hamilton, several staff members have confirmed that Megan appeared highly intoxicated. The video footage also showed her having some difficulty walking out of the dining room on her own."

"And Nate just left her on her own to get back to the room alone? Doesn't that seem a bit off to you, Captain?" I asked.

"I agree that Mr. Talbert, as a matter of moral responsibility, should have made sure your daughter got to her room safely. However, him not doing so is not a crime, no matter how strongly I feel about it personally," said Perez. "There is also another possibility we have to consider. Given your daughter's intoxicated state, it is possible that she had an accident," said Captain Perez, refusing to meet my gaze.

"An accident? What exactly are you suggesting, captain? Just come out and say it."

"Regrettably, there is a possibility that she may have fallen overboard. Due to the late hour, it would be unlikely that anyone would have witnessed her fall."

I was at a loss for words as I stared at him in disbelief. There was no way he could be serious. Megan had a deep fear of heights. She would never venture close enough to the deck railing to fall overboard. She wouldn't even sit on our balcony without first pulling the chair next to the sliding door.

"No. No way. Megan is scared to death of heights. She has refused to go anywhere near the deck rails the entire time we've been here. There is no way she would get close enough to fall overboard," I protested.

"She was drunk, Michelle. We have to consider it," responded Rochelle.

I stared at Rochelle, stunned.

"I cannot believe you right now. You know there is no way that happened."

Rochelle's face displayed a flicker of pity before she looked away.

"Ms. Hamilton, whether your daughter went overboard or left the ship of her own volition, I cannot say for certain at this time. I am still looking into the possibility of her going overboard. But for now we have concluded our search of the ship. Her lack of response to our announcements to pick up a courtesy phone suggests she is not aboard. That's the current reality of the situation we're facing."

"Yeah, well, screw reality. I'm choosing hope. I have to for my daughter's sake, as apparently I am her only chance. You've both given up on her."

I got up and walked to the door, opened it, and motioned for them to go.

"Michelle, I—please," Rochelle began, but I interrupted her.

"Don't bother, Rochelle. You've said more than enough this morning. Just go."

They walked out, neither of them willing to meet my gaze. I knew my daughter. She did not get off the ship alone in Mexico to find Brian. And she most certainly did not fall overboard.

Megan was on the ship. And I was going to find her. No matter what it took.

CHAPTER NINETEEN

Megan

My eyelids were heavy as they fluttered open. The room was pitch black except for the thin strip of light coming from under the door. My hip hurt from lying on the hard floor for. . . how long had it been? I struggled to remember how many days I had been held captive. Was it two days now? Three? Had the ship already left Mexico? I had no sense of time. Although I had no doubt that whatever was going to happen to me would be soon. We were scheduled to return to Los Angeles four days after the day I was first taken. It was reasonable that I would be passed on to my buyer while we were still in Mexico. Assuming I had been held for two days, they would have to release me from the ship sometime in the next twenty-four hours. Of course, I still had no way of determining if it was day or night. My judgment was based solely on the remaining fragments of my internal clock.

Dehydration was beginning to affect me. My tongue stuck to the roof of my mouth, so dry I was tempted to drink from the spiked water bottle that lay next to me. But if I wanted any hope of escaping again, I had to stay alert. Even a small amount of the water might dull my senses enough that I would miss an opportunity. Given my previous escape attempt, I was certain my captors would exercise greater caution from this point forward.

My head spun as I raised myself to a sitting position. With my hands tied behind me, my shoulders once again felt the agony. As I sat there, helpless, the minutes continued to tick by, and my attempts at devising a plan to save myself ended in failure. Tears streamed down my face, and I couldn't hold back my sobs. My emotions overwhelmed me as I sat there, crying, and releasing all the frustration and fear I had about my situation. It didn't help that it was so desolate below deck. I couldn't imagine there were thousands of people on the decks above me, eating, drinking, and laughing with no idea I was being held prisoner.

Sitting alone in the dark, crying, also gave me ample time to reflect on my life. I realized I had settled for Brian because I wanted that Instagram-able life everyone thinks they should have. In retrospect, we had never been a good match. Did it give me any solace to know he actually did me a favor by dumping me for another woman and running off to get married? Not even a little. But I was thankful that I no longer felt an inconsolable sadness when I thought of him. Our marriage was bound to end in divorce sooner or later, so it was a bullet dodged.

It took a while, but eventually I reached my breaking point and couldn't cry anymore. My exhaustion and dehydration were partly responsible, and I simply had no more tears left. That's when I decided there was no way I was getting off the ship. I'd rather die fighting than be sold to someone with such little regard for human life that they would buy another human being. The thought caused a surge of determination within me, confirming that I would not surrender. I would rather die here.

I was so lost in my thoughts that I didn't hear the door until it opened. I struggled to get on my feet, but I was too dizzy and lacked the strength. Nate walked into the room, bag in hand, as the lights flickered on.

"Enjoy your nap, Megan?"

My eyes narrowed as I glared at him.

He reached into the bag and pulled out a red sequined dress and heels. He tossed them at me, and I dodged to my left to avoid getting hit by a shoe.

What an asshole.

"Put these on. And there is makeup and a hairbrush in there too. Use them," he demanded, kicking the bag toward me. "I need you looking decent. Right now, you could almost pass for a tweaker. Not a good look on you, sweetheart."

I felt a surge of anger as I glanced at the dress and heels. Under no circumstances was I going to put on that getup. He could kiss my *entire* ass.

"There's a sandwich, chips, and a couple of sodas in there. Eat something before you pass out. Don't worry, it isn't laced with anything. Everything is unopened. I can't have you narced up when we hand you off, so no more sleeping pills. I'll be back in a few hours. Be ready to go."

I remained silent and turned my back on him.

"Don't be stupid, Megan. If you don't cooperate, things are only going to get worse for you. The best thing you can do now is just go along and get along. I don't care what you do once we hand you off. Be a bitch, try to escape, whatever. You won't be my problem anymore."

When I didn't respond, he moved nearer, reaching out and grabbing my chin, forcing me to face him. "Don't make me get ugly with you. Make no mistake—I will not hesitate to do so if I need to."

He pushed my face away, leaving my jaw sore from his grip. Then he reached into his pocket and pulled out a small retractable knife. He replaced my zip ties with looser ones, binding my hands in front of me instead of behind my back, which gave me the freedom to eat, apply makeup, and brush my hair. As he was leaving, he paused at the door and turned back to face me.

"A few hours Megan. Clean yourself up and be prepared to leave. You need to be ready for your trip."

My trip? That was a generous way to describe my abduction and pending sale into sex slavery. The door shut behind him, followed by the distinct sound of the lock.

Right away I grabbed the soda, water, and sandwich, inspecting them carefully. Seeing that they were sealed, I took a chance and dug in. I finished everything and took a moment to relax, feeling much better and more motivated.

I rummaged through the bag, looking for anything I could use as a weapon. A hairbrush and makeup. Nothing else. I tossed the bag down, frustrated. Then I picked up the red shoes and examined the heels.

I grinned as a plan took shape in my mind.

CHAPTER TWENTY

Michelle

I wasted no time grabbing my phone and wallet once Rochelle and the head of security were gone. I wrote a quick note to Megan, just in case she returned, and left to search for her.

I wandered around the decks, through the main dining rooms and ended up at the pool. Deep down, I knew Megan wouldn't be lounging at the pool, but I had to occupy myself until security finished reviewing the video from yesterday. Glancing around at the people on the deck, I envied their smiles and laughter. Unlike me, they weren't experiencing the pain of having their hearts ripped from their chests because their daughter was missing.

I took my phone out and brought up a recent picture of Megan. I went from table to table, showing Megan's picture to anyone willing to look, asking if they had seen her. The guests shook their heads, but promised to notify security if they spotted her. A lot of them asked me what had happened, and I told them of her disappearance. Many of the people I talked to were understanding, but not worried. But the fear was visible on a few of their faces when they heard my story. I was glad. I needed to stir things up. Security would rather I act like a sheep and trust that my daughter left the ship willingly or, even worse, fell overboard. But I had grown tired of playing the role of Mrs. Nice Guy. There must be someone who knew what happened to Megan. And I was determined to keep searching until I found that person.

I kept going until just after breakfast, taking a quick break to eat to maintain my strength for Megan's sake. I had no appetite at all. Eating was simply a means to keep myself going.

I hastily ate my meal and hurried back to my search, showing Megan's picture to every person I passed, but it didn't yield any results. Every place I searched left me with less hope than the last. I felt like I was treading water, just waiting to drown. I wandered into the atrium, unsure of how to proceed. Despite knowing it was likely pointless, I decided to check the room again. I was at a loss for what else to do. I had never felt so powerless in my life. The longer Megan was missing, the more I feared for her safety and well-being. Call it mother's intuition, but I knew she was in danger and that feeling became more urgent with each passing minute.

Upon returning to my empty cabin, I dialed Rochelle's room. Despite my recent defensiveness toward her, I still needed someone to talk this through with. And she *was* my closest friend. She was quick to answer the phone as soon as it rang.

"Hey. Is there any news about Megan?"

"No. I've been out all morning searching the ship and showing Megan's picture around. But no one has seen her. It's like she just disappeared into thin air."

My remark was met with silence. "I know what you're thinking, Rochelle, but you can't honestly believe she fell overboard, can you? You saw how she avoided the deck railings. There is no way she would get close enough to chance that. Even if she was drunk. I just don't believe that."

"I agree. I don't think she fell overboard. But Michelle, I think maybe she could have left the ship to look for Brian. I know you don't believe that, but I'm just trying to consider all the possibilities."

Listening to Rochelle, fear welled inside me. Megan could find herself in real danger if she got off the ship alone.

"Can you come to my room so we can try to figure this out?"

"Of course. I'll be right over."

I dried my eyes after hanging up. I had to stay strong, but it was hard to do. Rochelle's support was crucial, and I was grateful she was coming over. Five minutes passed before the knock at my door came. I swung the door open and stumbled into my best friend's embrace, sobbing.

"Shhhhh. It's okay, honey. We'll find her. Maybe we should go into Playa del Carmen this morning and show her picture around? It isn't as if we're sailing home tonight. We have time."

I wiped my eyes with the tissue Rochelle handed me, sniffing as I did so.

"Okay. That's a good idea."

I slung my purse over my shoulder, dropped my sea card inside, and made my way to the door. Rochelle followed me as we walked through the atrium and headed toward the exit. As we walked, I kept showing Megan's picture to fellow passengers, sharing that she disappeared during the cruise. The concern on their faces was clear, but I didn't care. I hoped people would start talking about my missing daughter. If making a scene about her vanishing would be beneficial, I was all in.

While walking along the main street in Playa del Carmen, we paused at vendor booths to show Megan's picture to the shopkeepers. By late morning, my discouragement had reached its peak.

"She didn't come here, Rochelle. I just know it."

"We don't know that, Michelle. No one on the ship had seen her either and we know she was there for two days before she went missing. Let's keep going a bit longer. Then at least we've covered all the bases."

I nodded in agreement and followed Rochelle to the next shop. I stuck with her plan until midafternoon. My intuition was screaming at me that my daughter was still on that ship, and I wanted to go back and look for her there.

"I'm ready to go back, Rochelle."

"Okay, listen. I think we should go to Costa Maya. We can catch a cab and be there in about an hour and a half. I found out where Brian is staying for his honeymoon."

My jaw dropped. "You tracked Brian down on his honeymoon? How would you even do that, Rochelle? And more troubling, *why* would you do that?"

"I called in a favor from an associate at a hotel down here. Listen, does it really matter how I found him? The point is, I say we go down there and see if he's seen Megan."

"We can just call him. What's the name of the hotel?"

"Don't be mad, but I tried to reach him yesterday. I couldn't get in touch with him then. They're probably out doing whatever. And who knows if the little pissant would even talk to us? Besides, if Megan was or is there, don't you want to be there so we can find her?"

"That's a good point. Okay, let's get going. We're burning daylight just standing around."

"Let me just go into that stand over there and get us some food to go and a couple of bottles of water. You flag us down a taxi and I'll be back in a few minutes."

Feeling hopeful for the first time in two days, I nodded at Rochelle. Maybe Megan really *did* go after Brian. While I didn't fully believe she would do it, I clung to that hope. I knew I had to pursue every possibility. Then if we knew she hadn't gone to Costa Maya, at least I would have confirmation she was still on the *Jewel of the Sea.*

CHAPTER TWENTY-ONE

Michelle

The back seat of the taxi was uncomfortably hot. I closed my eyes and lowered the window a little farther. A big part of me wished Megan had chased after Brian, giving me a trail to follow. A smaller part of me hoped she hadn't embarrassed herself like that. I didn't know how to feel. Worry consumed my mind, and I was grateful for Rochelle's leadership as I took a moment to gather my thoughts.

The taxi reached Costa Maya in record time thanks to our driver's formula one racing abilities and the lack of traffic. Sliding across the vinyl seat as the driver took a corner too fast, I noticed Rochelle grab the back of the passenger seat to steady herself.

"Good grief. I told him we wanted to get here in a hurry. I never told him to break every traffic law in the country," she snapped.

I took a quick look at her, but didn't respond. I lacked the energy for playful banter. I gazed at the scenery, wondering if Megan took this same path on her way to find Brian. I couldn't imagine what she would have been thinking. Megan had a practical, no-nonsense personality. She wasn't a woman who chased men or attempted to mend relationships after they were over. She might have had a hard time letting go of Brian because of their engagement, but it just didn't make sense to me she would run off without telling me. My thoughts kept returning to the same place. She would know I would be sick with worry. Although I acknowledged I irritated her at times, we had a close relationship, and she would never intentionally let me experience this kind of anxiety.

The driver spoke, and I snapped back to the present.

"We're almost there," said Rochelle.

I straightened up and noticed a cluster of buildings in the distance. The sparkling sea to my right and the lush resort landscaping created a picturesque view. A few minutes later, the taxi pulled up to the resort and came to an abrupt stop. Rochelle paid the driver, and we got out. Just as I turned to look at the glass entry doors, he sped away.

"Come on, let's go see if we can find the pissant," stated Rochelle, steering me inside.

The air conditioning was a welcome relief as I stepped into the lobby. Colorful pots filled with large banana plants dotted the space, with chairs arranged in circles for conversation.

"You wait here. Let me find out what room he's in."

I took a seat in one of the chairs, allowing the cool air to soothe my nerves as Rochelle approached the check-in desk. She promptly discovered Brian's room, and we rode the elevator to the third floor. I stood in front of room 302 and knocked on the door.

My knocking was met with silence. "Brian? It's Michelle Hamilton. I'm looking for Megan," I called out loudly.

Rochelle made another attempt, increasing the intensity of the knocks on the door.

"I don't think they're in there. Let's go look around the grounds," said Rochelle.

After taking the elevator to the lobby, we went in search of the pool. The space was large and packed with resort guests, and it took us almost fifteen minutes to move through it. There was no sign of Brian. Rochelle flagged down a waiter and asked for directions to the bar, and we made our way across the lawn to the other side of the resort.

"I hope he's not out on a boat excursion or snorkeling for the day or something. You know how he loves to do that kind of stuff," I griped.

"Well, he has to come back sometime. They are definitely checked in at the resort, so they'll be back at some point if they aren't here now."

As soon as we stepped into the open-air bar with a stunning ocean view, I caught sight of him. He was holding hands and laughing with someone I assumed was his new bride-to-be.

"Over there!" I exclaimed, pointing to the far corner of the bar.

We approached their table and stood there in silence, waiting for him to acknowledge our presence. He glanced in our direction and then did a double take. Confused, he looked back and forth between me and Rochelle.

"Michelle? What are you doing here?"

"We're looking for Megan. Has she been here, Brian? Have you seen her?"

"Megan? No. Why would she be here? I thought she was on a cruise."

"She was—she is. She's been missing for two days. No one has seen her. Security thinks she got off the ship at Playa del Carmen. Or that she fell overboard. I just know something is wrong, Brian. You know her as well as anyone. She would not get off the ship alone and she is afraid of heights. She wouldn't go near the side railings. Rochelle thought she might have come here looking for you."

"Looking for me? Why would she be looking for me?" He hesitated. "I'm here on my wedding trip," he said, glancing at his fiancée.

"Are you talking about Megan, your old girlfriend? Yeah, I think I would have definitely noticed if she was around," cringed Leticia, sipping her margarita and rolling her eyes.

"Let me handle this, babe," urged Brian.

Leticia nonchalantly shrugged and picked up her cellphone to keep herself busy. She struck me as someone who was completely self-centered. She and Brian were a perfect match and deserved each other.

"So you haven't heard from her?" asked Rochelle, as I continued to glare at Leticia.

"No. The last time I saw Megan was at her house, when I picked up the last of my things a couple of weeks ago."

I knew this would be a complete waste of time. I should have trusted my instincts. Now I had wasted the entire day chasing down a lead I knew was impossible. I sank into a nearby chair, burying my face in my hands.

In a soothing gesture, Rochelle placed her hands on my shoulders. "Thank you, Brian. Do you still have Michelle's number in case Megan shows up?"

"Sure. Is there anything else I can do to help?" he asked, kneeling in front of me.

I directed my gaze to his fiancée, who seemed utterly disinterested as she scrolled through her phone. I had to fight the temptation to slap her.

"I think you've done enough damage already, Brian," I sneered, as I stood to leave.

A look of guilt crossed his face as he lowered his head. I tried to summon some empathy for him, but my efforts fell flat. My top priority was finding Megan, which meant getting back to the *Jewel of the Sea.*

CHAPTER TWENTY-TWO

Michelle

The journey from Costa Maya back to Playa del Carmen seemed never-ending. Our taxi driver for the ride to the ship lacked the same sense of urgency as our first driver. When we finally arrived at the *Jewel of the Sea*, it was already late afternoon, and I could barely contain my anxiety.

I desperately needed to locate Captain Perez and tell him that Megan hadn't gone to Costa Maya in search of Brian; she had to be onboard the ship. We hurried onto the ship and rode the escalator up to the next level, where we made our way to the security office. We spent five minutes waiting in the outer office only to be informed that the captain was not in his office.

"Well, can you radio him or something? This is an urgent matter. My daughter has been missing for two days, and I have crucial information about her disappearance."

The security man hurriedly sent a message to his boss and got a reply within seconds.

"Captain Perez has asked that you head to your cabin and he will meet you there in thirty minutes."

"Tell him I'm on my way," I said, turning to leave.

I power-walked my way to the elevators. I was becoming increasingly frustrated by what I perceived as a lack of concern for Megan's disappearance.

"Try to be calm, Michelle. Making an enemy of security will not help anything," volunteered Rochelle.

"I want them to *do* something! There have been no organized interviews, nothing! No passenger announcements to be on the lookout for Megan. They searched the ship, he said, but who knows how thorough they were? *I'm* the one getting Megan's picture circulating among the passengers. Now that we know she didn't get off the ship, he has to do more."

"Okay, well, just take it down a notch. We need him to be on our side, not alienate him."

"No, Rochelle. I have been patient for long enough. I should have gotten more aggressive yesterday when my gut told me something was terribly wrong. I regret that now. And I will not stand idly by anymore while security does a half-assed job of searching for my daughter. They need to call in reinforcements!"

As we got closer to the elevators, Rochelle jogged to keep up with me. Once inside, she pulled me into a hug. "I'm going to stop by my room real fast and change and will be at your stateroom in fifteen minutes. I feel sticky from the heat today."

"Okay, I'll see you there," I said, stepping off the elevator.

Inside my room, I paced back and forth, unable to sit or relax. Rochelle arrived within the promised fifteen minutes, and we waited together for security to get there. A knock on the door came twenty minutes later.

Captain Perez and an unfamiliar security officer were waiting for me when I opened the door. I felt a sudden weight in my stomach as my heart plummeted.

Did they find Megan?

I clung to the doorframe for support.

"Did you find her?"

"No, Ms. Hamilton. This is officer Mateo Cortez, head of the team leading the search for your daughter."

Relief and sadness engulfed me in equal measure as I stepped aside. We found seats in the cabin, and I immediately turned to Captain Perez.

"We went to Costa Maya today. Megan has not been there. We spoke to her ex-fiancé, and he has not heard from her. We showed her picture to shopkeepers in Playa del Carmen and no one has seen her. She has to be on this ship."

"Ms. Hamilton, we reviewed the camera footage from our first day in Playa del Carmen and although we didn't spot Megan, it doesn't mean she didn't get off the ship. There are slightly over three thousand guests aboard, and the majority of them disembarked on the first day we docked in Mexico. We were hoping to see her on the video, but it's highly possible she got off the ship and we just can't locate her on the footage," replied Captain Perez.

"No. That makes no sense. She would not get off the ship alone. I'm telling you she is on this ship somewhere!" I cried.

"Ms. Hamilton, I have supervised the search for your daughter and she is not on board the ship. I personally searched the lower service decks in case she accidentally took a wrong turn and ended up down there and got lost. Our security staff is very thorough. I am certain she either disembarked from the ship or had an unfortunate mishap," said officer Cortez.

"She did not fall overboard! She is terrified of heights and wouldn't go near the railings. I have told you people this countless times," I argued.

"We have an overboard detection system with twelve sensor stations throughout the ship that use thermal cameras and micro radars to detect when someone has gone overboard. However, no alarm was activated on the night your daughter went missing. Also, none of our onboard cameras picked up anything unusual that night. Although we do not have 100 percent visibility in certain areas of the ship, based on our technology, I tend to agree with you she did not go overboard," theorized Captain Perez. "Also, our railings are designed with safety in mind and are pretty high. Passengers going overboard are almost always the result of an intentional act."

"Well, she most certainly was not suicidal! She was having a great time on the cruise. She had met Nate and was spending her time with him. Making plans for the following day with him, and in general, in good spirits," I reasoned.

"And because we are confident she is not on the ship, that only leaves her disembarking at Playa del Carmen," added officer Cortez.

"What if she's in someone's cabin being held hostage? You have to search the rooms," I cried.

"Ms. Hamilton, we cannot invade the privacy of our guests like that. We have no grounds to suggest she is being forcibly detained. There is no sign of foul play based on the evidence. All signs suggest that she voluntarily left the ship to go sightseeing."

"That's not true! You said her sea card hasn't been used, and you have no video proof that she left the ship. I've told you numerous times that she didn't want to go into Mexico with us. I want you to do something! Call the FBI."

"We are in international waters, Michelle. I don't think the FBI has the authority to swoop in and take over in Mexico," countered Rochelle.

It struck me as funny, in a twisted way, that I had never noticed Rochelle's pessimism before now.

"Actually, that's not true. International waters start twelve miles out from shore. The FBI *would* have jurisdiction in Mexico waters because your daughter is an American citizen and the *Jewel of the Sea* operates within the U.S. maritime dominion and admiralty of the United States, and sailed from a U.S. port. But once again, there is no evidence to suggest a crime has occurred. She is an adult who has the freedom to leave the ship and choose when or if to return," Captain Perez pointed out.

"No evidence of a crime? She is a missing American on *your* cruise ship. So I suggest you make that call, Captain Perez. Before I do. And my next call will be to the press," I threatened.

"As you wish, Ms. Hamilton. I can't promise an FBI investigation, but I will make the call. Before we go, there's something else I need to mention. I need you to leave the investigation to my staff and crew. Please refrain from involving other passengers by displaying your daughter's photo and claiming she has vanished. We have received complaints due to your interference in our investigation and the fear you are causing among the guests. If you don't stop, I will have no choice but to detain you."

"*Detain me?* You've got to be kidding me! I'm sorry if me searching for my missing daughter is making the other passengers uncomfortable. This is unbelievable," I chided, rising to pace again.

"Please, just let us do our jobs. I'll be in touch once I speak to the FBI," said Captain Perez.

I gave him a nod of understanding and decided to keep quiet. I could pretend to play nice with the security staff to avoid cruise jail, but you can sure as hell believe I was going to continue searching for my missing daughter.

CHAPTER TWENTY-THREE

Megan

I knew Nate would be back any time, and I anxiously paced the small, dark room, clutching a red shoe in each hand. I removed the plastic heel guards to reveal the steel tip point on both heels. They were the only weapons I had, and I was determined to use them to their fullest extent. I skipped applying any makeup, brushing my hair, and wearing the red dress. There was absolutely no way I was going to give in to Nate's demands.

I positioned myself behind the door, ready to attack, when I heard footsteps approaching. With a click, the lock was released and the door swung open. The lights flickered on just seconds later. Nate was the first one through the door. Just as I was about to strike his head with the first heel, my body froze when I saw someone else enter the room. My confusion was so overwhelming that I could only stare in disbelief. There I stood, hands in the air, clutching the shoes and gaping at them in bewilderment.

"Megan, really? Another escape attempt? I'm not pleased about what you did to my last man. Did you know you blinded him with that bleach? That's right. His eye tissue just kind of melted away. Dissolved into Jello. It was horrible, actually. Clever of you, but truly atrocious to see. I had to put him out of his misery, sadly. I have to say I really don't appreciate being one man down. And getting him overboard was frankly a hassle," said the person standing next to Nate.

Nate had yet to say anything. With a smug expression and a smile playing on his lips, he just stood there, thoroughly enjoying my state of shock. He quickly extended his arm and grabbed the shoes from me. I didn't have the power to resist him. I was unable to do anything except stare at the woman next to him.

"Rochelle? I don't understand," was all I could manage to whisper.

"Yes, Megan. It's me. You aren't hallucinating."

"But I don't understand." I repeated.

"Well, let me bring you up to speed, darling. I operate a highly profitable trafficking ring out of this ship. How did you think I made my money? My husband left it to me?" she asked, incredulously.

"He was a lazy waste of a man. He never could make a success of anything he tried. But I digress. I'm sorry I had to involve you in this. I genuinely am. Your mother is my closest friend, and I don't want to hurt either of you. But this is business. The sad truth is that one of the girls I had on hold from our most recent cruise met with an unfortunate accident, and I don't have time to vet another passenger. It's really quite a process, you know. Choosing girls who have no family or are traveling alone. It involves a significant amount of research. I needed a quick replacement, and there you were, heartbroken and in need of a vacation. You provided the perfect solution to my dilemma. My buyers are expecting ten girls, and I always meet my business commitments."

"No," I stated firmly, shaking my head. I was in complete denial, about as deep as one could possibly go.

"Oh, don't be so idealistic, Megan. We all have our secrets."

"You'll never get away with this," I answered.

"Well, it appears that I already have."

"My mother will never give up looking for me or trying to find out what happened to me. You know that."

"You make an excellent point, Megan. We both know how overprotective and domineering your mother tends to be. She's certainly very *extra* when it comes to you. Isn't that what you young people say nowadays? Extra?" She chuckled, and glanced at Nate. "Anyway, I've already laid the groundwork to take care of that. Your remains will be found burned beyond recognition in a taxi at the bottom of a ravine in Playa del Carmen, your purse and ID thrown from the wreckage, the apparent victim of a tragic car accident. You were evidently distraught and on your way to find Brian to beg him to change his mind about marrying Leticia. Anyway, I've already planted that seed in your mom's mind as the most plausible reason for your disappearance. Of course, I didn't count on her agreeing to go to Costa Maya to talk to that pissant Brian. By the way, if it makes you feel any better, his fiancée is a complete twit. But never mind that, a payoff to the local police and medical examiner and voilà! My problem was solved. The authorities will confirm it was you in the accident and everyone will move on. But don't worry, dear. I will be there for your mother during her grieving period."

"You're a psychopath, Rochelle."

"Perhaps," she conceded, shrugging. "But I can live with that. Now get changed and clean yourself up. Or I will let Nate and Mateo do it for you. And trust me, Mateo is, well, let's just say he can be handsy."

It wasn't until that point that I realized there was another man in the room. I had been so fixated on Rochelle that I failed to notice anything else. Mateo stepped forward, grinning. It was only then that I noticed his security nametag. A wave of nausea hit me, and the meal I had earlier was on the verge of making a reappearance.

"Go on, dear. Get changed and cleaned up. We're taking you off the ship in a few hours. Don't be shy. You're going to have to get comfortable undressing in front of strangers," said Rochelle, waving her hand in my direction.

I was frozen in place. Almost as if I was rooted to the ground. I just stood there staring at her in disbelief, realizing that the person I had considered an aunt for most of my life was behind my abduction. How did we never suspect that there was anything amiss? I couldn't help but be impressed by her ability to conceal her secret life.

Rochelle closed the distance between us, pausing mere inches from my face.

"Get changed and cleaned up, Megan. I will not ask you again."

My spine shivered as her voice's tone changed. At that moment, she was an altogether different person than the one I knew, and it jolted me into action. I moved to the corner of the room and faced away from them. I sensed their eyes on me as I slipped out of my evening gown and into the red sequined dress, and it sickened me. It was no surprise that Nate held on to the shoes. Once I had changed, I turned around to face my captors.

"That wasn't so hard, was it? Now, get some makeup on and do something with your hair, please. You're a beautiful girl, Megan, but right now you resemble something the cat drug home. I cannot turn you over to my buyers looking like this. Not for the money they're paying for you. And please, don't get any more cute ideas about escaping. Nate and Mateo will be right outside the door."

Nate led me to the far corner of the room and forced me to sit down while he put zip ties around my ankles, rendering me completely immobile. They left me there while Rochelle led the men out, and I was alone in the empty room once more. At least they left the lights on, which was a small consolation. The reality that Rochelle was behind my abduction hit me hard, and I was still trying to process it. I couldn't comprehend that she was the mastermind behind a human trafficking network. But the more I thought about it, the more things fell into place for me. She went on a lot of cruises. I'm not talking about a couple a year either. She went every other month. She claimed it was her addiction. Her way of seeing the world and meeting new people. But seriously, how can the average retiree afford to do that? Which led me to my next epiphany. Rochelle could afford to live in a massive home that was too spacious for her alone. She seemed to have an inexhaustible amount of money, which she credited to her late husband, though she never elaborated further. I had never considered questioning it before. Why would I? She never really got into details about what her husband did before he died. She would simplify his job by saying he dealt with stocks.

She had me and my mother both fooled, and the mere thought of my mom made my stomach churn all over again. If she refused to stop searching for me, would Rochelle pose a threat to her? Was it possible that she could uncover Rochelle's secret? There would only be one outcome for my mother if something like that were to happen. If Rochelle would sacrifice me, there was no doubt she would be a danger to my mom too.

The bottom line was that I couldn't allow them to take me off the ship. If I let that happen, I would stand no chance. My only possibility to get free would be during my transportation, and I had to be prepared for any opportunity that came my way. If I was lucky enough to get another chance to escape, I would have to use everything at my disposal.

CHAPTER TWENTY-FOUR

Michelle

Right after security and Rochelle left my cabin, I was alone with my thoughts, and that's when I broke down. I wept until my eyes were swollen. Megan's disappearance was something I took full responsibility for and I would never be able to forgive myself. She didn't want to come on this cruise, but my persistent nagging finally convinced her. My eyes swept across the empty stateroom and I shook my head. I recognized I was at fault, and I wouldn't abandon my quest to find her. I forced myself off the bed and doused my face with cold water. I looked terrible, with black circles under both eyes. Even though I seemed to have aged a decade overnight, I didn't have the energy to apply makeup. Finding Megan was the only thing that mattered.

I was about to leave the room when the bedside phone rang. Hoping that it might be an update about Megan, I hurriedly made my way to the table and sat on the bed as I answered.

"Hello?"

"Ms. Hamilton? It's Captain Perez, ship security. I have spoken to the FBI and would like to update you. May I come by your room?"

"Yes, of course. When?"

"Now, if it's not too inconvenient. This really can't wait."

"I'll be here," I confirmed, hanging up and speedily dialing Rochelle's cabin.

"Hey. You okay?"

"Yes. No. I don't know. Perez just called and said he spoke to the FBI and wants to give me an update. Can you come over? He sounded strange."

"Strange how?"

"I don't know. There was just something in his tone that frightened me. And he said this couldn't wait."

"Well, sure, I'll come over. But, Michelle, calm down. Your nerves are already on edge, so you're probably reading something into this that isn't there."

"Just hurry, please."

"I'm on my way."

It took Captain Perez twenty minutes to arrive while Rochelle and I waited together. By the time he knocked on the door, I had already lost hope that the FBI was going to help me and I was convinced I would have to start back at square one.

Taking a seat opposite us, the captain folded his hands in his lap and gazed downward. I could feel my heart pounding. His refusal to make eye contact frightened me.

"Captain Perez, what is it? What did the FBI say?"

"Ms. Hamilton, there is no easy way for me to say this. So please forgive my bluntness. The FBI has received reports of a deceased female in Playa del Carmen. She was the victim of a traffic accident on the road leading out of the city, where the wreckage was found at the bottom of a ravine. The fire destroyed everything, and the remains were unidentifiable. However, a handbag was discovered nearby, possibly thrown from the vehicle upon impact. It contained your daughter's wallet and ID."

I let out a gasp and stood up. "No! It isn't her. She wouldn't be driving out of Playa del Carmen. Someone must have stolen her purse."

"Yes, that is obviously a possibility. But whoever this is, she was in possession of your daughter's ID. After my call to the FBI to report a missing passenger, the agent in charge notified me of the unidentified accident victim. The police in Playa del Carmen had already notified the local police in your city based on the ID found at the accident site. In turn, the FBI was notified, and when the agent assigned to the case was unable to contact any next of kin, he located your daughter's dental records and sent them to the medical examiner in Playa del Carmen. That will confirm the accident victim's identity either way. I regret having to inform you of this news, Ms. Hamilton."

A sob escaped me, and Rochelle stood to gather me into an embrace. My mind reeled as my insides shredded at the thought of what Megan might have suffered. I couldn't believe this was happening, and I didn't realize the unnatural keening sounds I heard were coming from me. I crumpled onto the bed, Rochelle's arms still wrapped around me.

"Please, call the ship's doctor," I heard Rochelle say.

Captain Perez spoke into the radio clipped to his belt as I sobbed uncontrollably. Rochelle attempted to calm me, but I could only respond with more wailing. I felt like my heart was shattering into a thousand pieces.

"Shhhh. You're probably right. Someone stole her purse. It's not our girl. She's going to be okay. We'll find her," she kept repeating to me.

But I wasn't really hearing what she was saying. My mind ran riot with the possibilities. How would I survive if it was my daughter lying at the bottom of that ravine? As the shock set in, time seemed to slow down, and I did not resist when the doctor arrived to sedate me. I didn't have the strength to.

Rochelle was sitting in the chair next to my bed when I woke up several hours later. I propped myself up and scanned my surroundings, filled with confusion. But reality came crashing down hard on me when I was suddenly reminded of Captain Perez's visit.

"How long have I been asleep?"

"Not nearly long enough."

"What time is it?"

Rochelle glanced at the bedside clock. "Early. It's only seven o'clock."

"Have you been here all night?"

"Of course. I wouldn't leave you alone."

"We sail for home this evening. I need to contact the medical examiner in Playa del Carmen," I said, sitting up.

"Captain Perez is going to do that, Michelle. The FBI is handling things. He will call us the minute they know something."

I collapsed back onto the bed, defeated. Rochelle was right. I had no choice but to wait.

"Michelle, I'm sorry to say this, but maybe it's time that you accepted the possibility that it might have been Megan in that car accident. Security has searched the ship, and she's not on board."

I stared at Rochelle in shock. I couldn't believe she said that to me when just last night she reassured me it wasn't Megan lying in the morgue. She seemed so indifferent this morning. Cold, somehow. It was like she wasn't talking about my daughter, the same person she considered her niece. How could she just give up on Megan like that? Suddenly, the space between us felt much too wide, and the first seeds of doubt were planted in my mind. When I didn't respond, she changed the subject.

"Anyway, you need to eat something. I'm going to go get us something from the buffet. I'll be quick. Just rest until I get back."

"I can't eat anything, Rochelle. Get something for yourself."

"You have to eat, Michelle. Stay here, and I'll be back before you know it."

I sat up, unsure of what else to do. I had a sense of being trapped in someone else's nightmare with no way to break free. I was considering telling Rochelle I would go with her, but she grabbed her purse and left before I could say anything. It was just as well. Some space from her would do me good, and I needed to get out of the room, if only for a few minutes. I longed for a change of scenery and some fresh air to clear my mind.

I splashed cold water on my face again, which seemed to be the sum of my self-care regime for the past couple of days. Since I was a few minutes behind Rochelle, that would guarantee me some much-needed time to myself. I could at least stand on the deck and take in the salty air. The sedative from the doctor last night had left me feeling sluggish, and I needed to have a clear head. I had to plan what to do next, because I was certain my daughter had not perished in that car accident. I would just know it if she was gone. I trusted my instincts.

Turning the corner at the end of the hall, I stopped dead in my tracks. Rochelle and Nate were standing next to each other, both with their backs turned toward me, their heads together. When did they become so friendly, I wondered? I sensed something was off and immediately ducked behind the wall, making sure I couldn't be seen. The volume of their voices increased as their conversation grew more intense.

"We should have done this last night, Rochelle. We are taking a huge risk doing it today. Plus, the ship sails tonight, so our window is decidedly limited."

"Do you think I don't know that, Nate? I realize taking Megan as a replacement isn't ideal. Do you think I really want to include my friend's daughter in my trafficking sale? I don't. But I honestly don't have any other choice at this point. The people we sell to are expecting to get what they paid for. Which is ten girls. Plus, there were things beyond my control happening last night. How would it look if Michelle had woken up, and I wasn't there with her? She is right where we need her to be, and her getting suspicious would merely complicate things further."

"Well, now we have bigger problems, don't we?"

"You work for me, Nate. Remember that. Just get Megan off the ship today. I don't care how you do it. That's what I pay you for. So go do your job and get her to the trap house so the runners can keep her in check until the buyers arrive to pick her up with the rest of the girls. Tell her if she resists or tries to escape again, her mother will die. She won't give us any more trouble."

"I hope you're right. Because that bitch is testing the last of my patience."

"Just go. I have to get breakfast and get back to the room. Once Michelle finds out the medical examiner has confirmed to the FBI that the dental records of the accident victim match Megan's, she is going to completely unravel, and what little composure she has left is going to fly right out the window. By the way, did you have the rest of the payment delivered to our doctor friend?"

"Yes. Our contact at the police department and the medical examiner have both been paid in full. Everything is in place. They will confirm it was Megan in the burned taxi. That should keep ship security and the FBI off our backs."

"Okay, good. Go make this happen. We don't need the FBI sniffing around. I'll keep Michelle busy. I'm going to call the ship's doctor and ask that he sedate her again, so she stays out of the way."

I felt anchored in place after hearing the bombshell Rochelle had just delivered. I leaned on the wall for support as sudden dizziness threatened to overtake me. My mind couldn't process what I had just heard, my heart racing in my chest. As I stood there in the hallway, I grappled with the realization that my best friend was behind my daughter's disappearance. It was then that I recognized what other information I had gathered. Megan was alive! She was on the ship. Rochelle told Nate to get her off the ship this morning. They obviously bribed the medical examiner and police to say it was Megan in the car wreck.

After the initial shock subsided, an unfamiliar anger boiled within me. My head was suddenly clear, and I spun around and sprinted back to my room. Once inside, I immediately locked and bolted the door, then rushed to the phone by the bedside to call Captain Perez.

CHAPTER TWENTY-FIVE

Michelle

My hands trembled as I dialed the security office.

"Security, Houghton speaking."

"Yes, I need to speak to Captain Perez immediately. It's an emergency. This is Michelle Hamilton."

"Hold for Perez."

I waited anxiously for the captain to answer the call, while every second felt like an eternity.

"Hello, Ms. Hamilton. My officer said this was an emergency. What's the problem?"

"Megan is on the ship. I have proof. I need to meet you. But not in my cabin. Rochelle will be back here soon, and I need to speak to you alone."

"Ms. Hamilton, I'm still waiting for a call from the FBI once the medical examiner has completed his dental exam. I'm expecting to hear from them sometime this morning. I understand it's difficult to be patient, but with no updates, we are at a standstill."

"Please, Mr. Perez, just give me ten minutes. You're going to want to hear this, I promise. And we don't have much time before she is going to be taken off the ship," I cried, a small sob escaping me.

Captain Perez let out a heavy sigh, and I could tell he was simply humoring me. I didn't care. All I needed was for him to listen and agree to meet me right away.

"Can you meet me in the Bistro dining room? I can be there in ten minutes," he said.

"Be there in five, Captain. My daughter's survival hinges on it."

I hung up before he could respond. To prevent Rochelle from suspecting that I was aware of her actions, I scribbled a note and taped it to the door before I left.

Needed some air. Be back later. Don't worry about me. I just want some time alone to process things.
Michelle

I hurried to the Bistro dining room as fast as I could. Within five minutes, I arrived and settled at a table in the back, away from other passengers, to ensure our conversation would be private. I fidgeted nervously while the waiter took my order for a black coffee. Despite my nerves not needing the extra caffeine coursing through my system, I still felt a little groggy due to the lingering effects of the sedative.

Captain Perez appeared at the entrance of the dining room and scanned the tables. I waved at him just as he caught sight of me. He weaved his way around the diners and reached the table as the waiter arrived with my coffee.

"I'll have a coffee as well, please," he said, nodding to the waiter.

Resting his hands on the table, he locked eyes with me, patiently awaiting my explanation for insisting that he meet me. I steadied myself by taking a deep breath before I started.

"Captain, this is going to sound strange. But it's important to me you know I am not crazy before I share this information with you. My mind is clear and I am absolutely rational. I am not fantasizing or manifesting anything."

"All right. Duly noted."

"This morning, I stepped out of my room for some fresh air, hoping to catch a few minutes to myself. Rochelle had just left to get us breakfast from the buffet. I came across her and Nate, my daughter's recent acquaintance, in a nearby hallway looking quite friendly. It was a surprise for me to see them together, because as far as I knew, like me, Rochelle had only met Nate a couple of times. Both of them were unaware of my presence, and I made sure I stayed out of sight. But I could hear their conversation very clearly."

"Continue, please. Tell me exactly what you heard."

And so I did. I talked him through the details of Rochelle and Nate's exchange, the words tumbling out. My voice cracked as I recounted the terrifying moment when I realized they were responsible for Megan's disappearance. The moment I finished, the waiter was back with the captain's coffee.

"Sorry about the delay. We had to make more. Big run on the coffee this morning," he said, smiling.

"It's fine, thank you," replied the captain.

Perez mixed cream and sugar into his cup, his brows drawn together deep in thought.

"Say something, please," I begged.

He laid his spoon on the saucer and leveled his gaze at me.

"I'm unsure how to respond to that, Ms. Hamilton. If what you say is true, then we are facing a major issue that requires immediate action, obviously."

"It *is* true, Captain. I have no reason to accuse my friend of twenty years of something so vile. I can hardly believe it myself, and honestly, I probably wouldn't believe it unless I had heard it firsthand. I understand you might think I'm desperate for another outcome other than the car accident. That I'm a grieving mother refusing to accept that my daughter is lying in a morgue in Mexico. That I'm clinging to any other hope than the truth. But let me assure you, that is not the case. So many things make sense to me now. Rochelle's insistence that Megan went to Costa Maya, for example. She knows Megan would never do that. All I am asking for is your help in monitoring the exits when they open this morning for our final visit to Mexico."

Perez gazed out the dining room window at the port of Playa del Carmen. The water sparkled like a sapphire as the early morning sun reflected on it.

"Why not just confront them?" he asked.

"Because I know Rochelle. Well, obviously I don't. But I know her well enough to realize that she would never just confess to us. That would be stupid of her, and Rochelle is anything but stupid. Plus, if they know we are aware of their plans, they might escalate matters. Or panic and harm Megan."

"Fair enough. But the FBI will never get here in time. The exits open for passengers in an hour."

"I know. It will come down to me and you, and any of your staff you can assign. Is there any other way off the ship except the main boarding areas? A staff exit?"

"There are exits on both sides of the ship, port and starboard. Staff and crew use the same gateways as passengers. However, there will be no permission granted to staff or crew to leave the ship today as we depart for Los Angeles this evening."

"So we have two exits to cover, then. I'm not sure how they plan to remove Megan from the ship. She wouldn't cooperate and simply walk off with them. I'm certain of that much. Can you send an officer with me to one exit?"

"Ms. Hamilton, if I agree to this, I need your word that if we find nothing, then you will let this go and wait for the medical report from the FBI. The bureau's assessment of the evidence at the accident scene suggests your daughter has likely been located, so I cannot allocate any additional resources to her disappearance. At least not until we have a definitive outcome. I will assist you strictly as a courtesy, as it seems you are convinced of what you heard this morning. Personally, I feel you may have misconstrued the conversation. Despite that, I am prepared to give you the benefit of the doubt."

"Thank you, Captain! That's all I am asking of you. But I'm right about this. I am. You'll see."

Perez acknowledged me with a nod, but his expression was clouded with doubt. I didn't let it bother me. I was determined to bring Megan back and make sure Rochelle and Nate faced the consequences, no matter the cost. I'd do whatever it took, even sell my soul, to save my daughter.

"Give me a moment to make a phone call. We can monitor the main exit while I station two officers at the other exit. If Megan is aboard the ship and someone attempts to remove her, we will know."

He stepped a couple of feet away, but I could still hear his side of the conversation.

"I need you to check something out for me. There are two passengers onboard I need information on. Rochelle Kendrick and Nate Talbert. I need you to check the system and see if they've been on any other cruises, and if so, I want the dates and where they traveled. I want to know if they have been on any of our cruises at the same time."

I sighed with relief. The captain was finally taking me seriously, and it seemed like I was making headway in finding Megan. All I needed to do now was avoid Rochelle. Rochelle, the woman who had been my closest friend for the past twenty years. The woman who was willing to offer my daughter for sale. And for what? To finance her human trafficking operation for her own gain? It was disgusting.

I never thought I could feel such hatred toward another human being as I did at that moment. But I realized it just wasn't true. I was absolutely capable of such strong feelings. Most of us would do anything to save our child. Me included.

CHAPTER TWENTY-SIX

Megan

I always thought when you died, your life was supposed to flash before your eyes. That didn't happen to me. Although this wasn't the exact moment of my death, I thought I would have some remorse for the choices I wished I had made differently. But then again, what was truly worth remembering about my life? Besides a failed engagement, I had little going on except for being a kindergarten teacher. And then I ended up in this place. Where my mother's best friend was about to sell me into a human trafficking operation while I was trapped on a cruise ship. That pretty much covered the main points. The worst part of it was I couldn't understand how I ended up in this mess. The situation was so unbelievable that it would have been laughable if not for the very real danger I faced.

I tugged at the red sequined dress with my bound hands. It was both itchy and uncomfortably tight. Squirming around on the floor caused the dress to twist, making it even more constricting. Leaning against the wall, I let out a scream of frustration. There was a loud bang on the door in response, confirming that Rochelle had indeed left a guard outside the door, as promised.

The red shoes would be perfect weapons, but since Nate had confiscated them, there wasn't much else I could do. They had to take me off the ship to get me into Mexico, and that thought gave me a glimmer of hope. I may not be able to escape now, but surely we would be in the public eye at some point. Then I could undoubtedly draw public attention when we disembarked and made our way to our final destination. I would have to make my move then. I would scream at the top of my lungs and create a scene. I always told my students if they were being taken against their will to scream "This is not my mom!" or "This is not my dad!" That way, people would know they weren't just a child having a tantrum. I planned on using the same tactic. I would shout that I didn't know these people, and they were abducting me. That should catch someone's attention. It seemed to be the only play I had left. Even if I could still use the red heels as a weapon and had them with me, being bound would stop me from running.

The minutes ticked by as I anxiously waited for something to happen, my nerves on fire. It wasn't long before I heard the familiar lock click, and fear surged through me like an electrical shock. With a bottle of water in hand, Nate entered the room and made his way toward me in the corner.

"Drink it," he demanded, holding out the bottle of water.

Oh no. Not another round of sleeping pills.

"I'm not thirsty. I feel nauseous. I don't think I can even keep water down."

"Well, you'd better figure out how you're going to make that happen, Megan. It's time for a nap."

I had hoped this wouldn't happen, believing Nate was being truthful when he said I wouldn't be drugged again. But obviously they were going to. They had to realize I wouldn't just walk off the ship quietly with them. I couldn't believe I hadn't thought of it earlier, but it made complete sense. To avoid attracting attention, they would need me to be quiet and cooperative, and undeniably, I had been neither of those things up to that point.

When I didn't immediately reach for the water, Nate yanked my head back and forcefully poured liquid into my mouth as I attempted to scream. I gagged and sputtered, as if I was being waterboarded. I ingested enough of the water for me to understand further fighting would be pointless. In less than ten minutes, my eyes grew heavy, and I could feel myself slipping into darkness. My last thought was that when I woke up again, it would already be too late for me to do anything to save myself.

CHAPTER TWENTY-SEVEN

Michelle

I was on edge as Captain Perez and I waited at the starboard exit. All around us, staff and crew were busy preparing for the influx of people disembarking for their final visit to Mexico. I was nervous and fidgety, fearing that we would somehow overlook Megan's departure from the ship. Or worse yet, she might be at the port side exit without being seen by the security posted there. Taking the risk of catching someone in the act of abducting her was a huge gamble, but confronting Rochelle and Nate would only tip them off we were aware of their involvement. And I couldn't take the chance of allowing them to execute their plan because they panicked at being caught out. I also couldn't be sure either of them would be the one to transport her off the ship. It made sense that they would have other people on board helping them.

As the opening of the exits grew closer, people lined up to get off the ship into Mexico. Captain Perez maintained continuous communication with security at the alternate exit. I scanned the bustling crowds, hoping to find any signs of something or someone suspicious, but all I could see were swarms of tourists eager to explore Playa del Carmen. As the massive doors swung open, a wall of people surged toward us. The crew needed time to scan each passenger's sea card before they could leave, and that allowed me to observe everyone passing through.

Fear crept in when an hour passed with no sign of Megan. I worried she had slipped by me or that they were transporting her off the ship through another means. It would be so easy to miss her. People moved in and out of line, kids ran around, making the crowd a constantly moving puzzle. Captain Perez assured me that if anyone were to disembark, they would have to use one of the designated exits. I hoped he was right. I doubted the vigilance of the security staff posted on the port side of the ship, but what other choice did I have? It was impossible for me to be in two places at one time.

As time dragged on, I started to believe that we should have confronted Rochelle and Nate after all. What if they successfully removed Megan from the ship? If that were the case, I'd be completely powerless. I was absolutely clueless about what I was doing. I didn't deal with criminals and kidnappers. Plus, I didn't know what Rochelle might be capable of. Captain Perez had more knowledge in that area than me, yet I suspected he was just along to placate me and prove me wrong. Unlike me, he didn't hear the coldness in Rochelle's voice. I now had no doubt that I couldn't trust her.

Just as I was about to suggest we switch gears and start searching for Rochelle and Nate, Perez insisted I go outside for some fresh air.

"Ms. Hamilton, please don't take this the wrong way, but you are making me anxious. I know this is stressful, but please. It might be beneficial for us both if you just took a moment to get some fresh air and tried to calm down. Take a quick walk around the deck outside."

Without waiting for my response, he led me to the front of the line.

"Ma'am, you'll have to join the line at the back," said the bored employee working the exit, gesturing to the long line of people waiting to leave.

There were murmurs from a few people behind me as they witnessed me trying to jump ahead of them in line.

Captain Perez took a step forward. "Ms. Hamilton is with me, and I'm authorizing her immediate access off the ship."

While I rummaged through my purse for my sea card, he passed her his crew member card. She scanned our cards and waved me through. I was ready to jump out of my skin.

Once I was outside, I stood at the edge of the walkway and watched passengers leaving for a day of sightseeing in Mexico. For twenty minutes, I observed the crowd, hoping to spot Megan. I hadn't seen anything unusual until my gaze landed on a woman in a wheelchair. Her features were concealed by the floppy straw hat, face mask, and oversized sunglasses she wore, but the man pushing her seemed oddly familiar as he lifted his face to glance upward. His baseball cap was pulled low on his forehead, as his eyes anxiously surveyed the crowd, darting from one person to another. As I examined the woman in the chair, the hairs on the back of my neck stood on end. She was wrapped in a blanket, seemingly asleep, with her head tilted to the side, resting on the chair's backrest. They reached the dock's edge, where a row of taxis and Ubers were waiting to transport people to the city. The man angled his head downward, although it was unnecessary. No one bothered to pay any attention to him or the woman in the wheelchair. A nagging feeling tugged at the back of my mind. I couldn't place him, but I was sure we had crossed paths before, and it was bothering me. It would be very unlikely that I would recall the face of a fellow passenger. Therefore, I must have interacted with him in some other way. My mind filtered through all the waiters and crew members I had been in contact with, but nothing stood out to me. Besides the security staff, I hadn't really spoken much to any other crew members. As I connected the dots, a mental image emerged. He was the security officer who had come to my cabin with Captain Perez. I drew a blank, trying to recall his name. Marcelo? Mauricio something? Suddenly, it hit me. Mateo. Mateo Cortez.

I gasped and hurried back toward the exit. There was no time to wait for a scan to get back inside. I waved my arms wildly in the air like a madwoman, calling for Perez. Unsurprisingly, it didn't take long for the captain to look in my direction. With a swift stride, he approached me wearing a very displeased expression.

"Ms. Hamilton. What is the matter now?" he asked, guiding me away from the exit.

I grabbed his arm. "You said no staff or crew were allowed to exit the ship today, right?"

"That's correct."

"I just saw Officer Cortez pushing a woman in a wheelchair off the ship. It took me a moment to realize who it was. They must have come out from the other exit. The woman looked like she was asleep. She was covered in a blanket, with a huge hat and mask, and large sunglasses on, so I couldn't see her face. But even though Cortez had a hat on, I knew I recognized him from somewhere. That could be Megan in the wheelchair!"

When I looked back at the dock, they were no longer in sight.

"Please, you have to believe me! They were down there, right by the taxi line. Why would he be getting off the ship with a woman in a wheelchair? They may have drugged her or something."

I tugged on his arm, signaling him to follow me toward the exit. The crowd of passengers slowed our progress as we rushed down the ramp. I stopped at the bottom near the dock, carefully surveying the surroundings for any sign of the man pushing the wheelchair. Captain Perez stood alongside me, blocking the morning sun with his hand.

"There!" he blurted out, pointing to a van with its emergency flashers blinking.

I watched helplessly as Cortez carried the woman from the wheelchair and placed her inside a white van with darkly tinted windows. Disregarding the wheelchair, he let it roll freely across the deck where it went unnoticed as people sidestepped around it. My heart quickened as Cortez climbed into the van and pulled the side panel shut.

"Let's go," said Perez, as he gripped my hand and urged me forward toward the van.

We ran across the dock, dodging the people in our path. The van started moving away. The mob of pedestrians forced the van to slow to just a few miles per hour, but it felt like an eternity to reach the end of the dock where it met the pavement. Due to my height and the crowds, I kept losing sight of the van. Perez kept moving, and I trailed behind him without hesitation.

We came to a stop in the street just as the van eased out into traffic. Taxis and Ubers crowded the street, creating a traffic jam, but the van had maneuvered past and disappeared from sight. Despite being out of breath, I kept going. Perez flagged down a taxi and we climbed into the back seat. He directed the driver in Spanish, as the driver did his best to navigate through the gridlock of vehicles.

Several minutes passed before we finally exited the parking lot. It took all my strength not to scream at the driver to hurry. I searched the street in both directions, but the white van was nowhere to be found, and a sense of hopelessness flooded me. I was convinced Megan was in that van, and we may have just missed our one opportunity to locate her alive.

My nerves were already on edge when the sound of Perez's phone startled me further. He withdrew it from his pocket and checked the screen, then immediately answered.

"What did you find out? Are you sure? Freeze both of their sea cards for exit access immediately. They are not to leave the ship under any circumstance. And let me know if either of them tries to disembark. If they attempt to leave and don't comply with the restriction on their sea cards, detain them immediately. In the meantime, I need covert eyes on both of them until further notice. Thank you. Good work, Simpson."

I waited anxiously as he hung up and shifted in the seat to face me. "Rochelle and Nate have been on eight of the same cruises in the last eighteen months. That averages out to once every other month.

That's far too many coinciding travel times to be a coincidence. They're definitely working together."

Even though my suspicions were now justified to Perez, I was more terrified than ever. Just how large was this operation and where were they taking my daughter?

CHAPTER TWENTY-EIGHT

Megan

I had to take back everything I said before. There were worse things that could have happened to me than being held captive on the ship. As it turned out, being separated from three thousand or so potential rescuers on that ship was definitely worse.

A pothole jolted the vehicle I was in, causing my eyes to flutter open momentarily. I was in something larger than a car, but I couldn't discern any further details. Mateo was on the other end of the seat from me, his gaze fixed on the scenery outside the window. I wanted to remain alert, but my eyes were so heavy. I allowed them to close, but battled to remain conscious. I didn't dare to look around, assuming it was just me, the driver, and Mateo in the vehicle. That wasn't ideal. Two men would have no trouble overpowering me, especially in my current state. I adjusted my legs slightly and could tell they were no longer restrained. I knew my hands were no longer in zip ties, and that was a promising start.

As the haze in my mind cleared, I cautiously peeked to see my surroundings while Mateo was occupied, gazing out the other window. All I saw were trees and overgrown tropical plants. The landscape had a jungle-like quality, making me think we were in a deeply remote location. The highway was dotted with small houses and a few livestock in areas cleared from the overgrowth, but no gas stations or other signs of a town were in sight.

I was totally clueless about the conversation between Mateo and the driver, who were speaking in Spanish. Laughter punctuated the conversation every so often, and they didn't seem to be on high alert. I was sure they felt at ease, thinking I posed no threat to them while I was still unconscious. Even when I was awake, they likely didn't view me as dangerous. I could feel the red heels on my feet as I wiggled my toes. They were my only weapon, and I had no qualms about using them to neutralize Mateo and the van driver. I was indecisive though, and unsure about the right choice. Should I take a chance and make a move now, while it was just the three of us? Maybe I could disable Mateo first, then the driver, take the van, and make a getaway. If the driver crashed the van during the fight, I would still be stuck with either two dead, injured, or very ticked-off captors. Plus, I was thoroughly disoriented and had no idea where I was. I had neither money nor a phone. And given my lack of proficiency with the Spanish language, communication with others would be spotty at best. Then again, I also didn't know where they were taking me or what lay ahead once I got there.

I might not get another opportunity to escape. This could turn out to be my best chance yet. While psyching myself up for the fight, I noticed the vehicle beginning to slow down. Mateo spoke to the driver, and we made a sharp turn.

No!

I had wasted too much time pondering my next move, and now we were going to stop. My chest thumped with my pounding heart. Was someone here ready to take possession of me? Or was it just a holding location? I closed my eyes and tried to control my breathing to avoid giving away that I was awake. The vehicle came to a halt and someone tapped on the glass. I listened as the front window powered down and the driver spoke a few words to someone outside. We moved forward again, and I stole a glance without Mateo noticing. We were at a seemingly ordinary house, indistinguishable from the others we had passed, except this house had two guards patrolling the perimeter, each carrying a rifle slung over his shoulder. That wasn't a good sign.

The van stopped in front of the house, and Mateo slid open the panel door. He gave my shoulder a shake.

"Hey. You awake?"

I didn't respond. I listened to my gut and maintained the illusion of being unconscious. That was the only edge I had. Mateo let out a sigh and muttered a curse before reaching over to lift me up and awkwardly carry me out of the van. He came to a stop and readjusted my position, and I let my limbs dangle limply at my side. I inhaled the dust stirred up by the van's departing tires as I listened to it start up and drive away. That left one less person. So far, I knew there were at least three men here. Mateo, along with the two guards. There might be additional guards stationed elsewhere or others inside the house, but I knew for certain there were at least three of them. Those odds didn't sit well with me.

Despite my being nearly a foot shorter and significantly lighter than Mateo, he still struggled to carry me. He used his knee to support my weight while he opened the front door with one hand. He crossed the threshold while I listened closely for any sign of others. Silence greeted us, and Mateo didn't call out for anyone. We encountered another door and Mateo cursed while he fumbled to open it. The sound of a light switch being flipped on signaled the sudden arrival of light, and even though my eyes were closed, I could sense the change in brightness. I could tell we were descending stairs as Mateo advanced. As soon as we entered the basement, I was hit by the strong stench of urine and heard what sounded like chains clinking. I lifted one eyelid and discovered a single bulb hanging from the ceiling on the left side, casting light into the corner of the room. I decided it was best not to risk moving my head to look around. Mateo was fully concentrated on carrying me, oblivious to my slight backward leg movement. I reached down and slipped off one of my heels, clutching it tightly and concealing it behind my back.

I took a deep breath and counted to three in my head. Then, with one swift move, I swung my arm up and over my body, connecting the pointed heel of the shoe with Mateo's temple. I let go of the shoe, but it was still stuck in his skull. Letting out a grunt, he promptly released his grip on me. I only had a millisecond to realize that was bad news for Mateo before I collided with the rising concrete floor. I landed on my hip with a sickening thud, sending my other shoe skidding across the basement floor on impact. The fall knocked the wind out of me and left me gasping for air as I fought to catch my breath. Mateo lay motionless in a heap beside me. I ignored the pain and hastily scrambled to my knees, unable to stand yet, feeling dizzy and fearing I might faint, but I forced myself to push through. Mateo had a gun and a flashlight tucked into his waistband, and I wasted no time in snatching both. Now in my bare feet, I rapidly moved away, pressing against a wall while keeping the gun pointed at him. He remained motionless on the floor; the red shoe imbedded in the side of his head. I hesitated before standing up and taking a tentative step closer to him. I nudged his side with my foot, but he didn't react. Crouching down, I placed a finger on his neck, finding no pulse.

Oh my God. I killed him.

I took two steps back and hunched over, feeling the urge to vomit.

I was wrong before, when I said that being taken off the ship was the worst thing that could happen. It seemed I hadn't allowed the situation to reach its peak yet. I was in a basement in the middle of nowhere, in Mexico, with no phone, no transportation, at least two armed guards outside, and my high heel lodged in my abductor's skull. There was no question that I was smack in the middle of the worst-case scenario. I mean, what else could possibly go wrong?

Okay, yes, he was kidnapping me. But I hadn't intended to kill him. I just wanted to disable him right away so I could escape. I leaned against the wall for support, facing away from his dead body.

I took slow, controlled breaths to calm myself. At least I had a gun now. Maybe I could defend myself. It wasn't like I knew how to shoot it, but it was still something. Maybe there was a chance I could slip past the two guards unnoticed. But how would I get away? I hadn't spotted any other vehicles when we arrived, and I was armed with a weapon I didn't have the first clue how to use. I couldn't be certain about the number of people I would be going up against, and I had no plan in place. Besides all that, I had to navigate through the jungle to safety wearing a tight, short cocktail dress and one high heel, because there was no way I was going to pull my other shoe out of Mateo's temple. I felt like I might hyperventilate. Or be sick again. It was then that the tears came, serving as a release more than anything else. I pushed away from the wall, pivoted toward the stairs, and got as far as two steps before a voice made me jump. I froze, listening in the dark.

"Hey, hello? A little help here, please?"

The woman's voice seemed to come from the corner of the room. I spun around abruptly and lost my grip on the flashlight. My hands shook as I picked it up, turned it on, and pointed it in the direction the voice had come from.

The sight before me caused me to gasp and almost drop the flashlight again. Nine women sat on filthy mattresses on the concrete, their ankles shackled to the wall by short chains. Shielding their eyes, they blinked in response to the light.

"Hi there," greeted the same voice, giving me a little wave. "Nice work with Mateo, by the way. Can you get his keys and unlock us, please?" she asked.

Her hair, blonde and matted, clung to one side of her head while traces of old mascara were visible under her eyes. I glanced at the other women, who were all in similar condition. They were young and dressed like me, but their short cocktail dresses had definitely seen better days. It looked like they had been held prisoner here for a while. The sight of them left me so shocked that I couldn't utter a word, so I just continued to stare stupidly at them.

"Um, listen, I know you just went through something here, but we could really use your help. So, if you could just *fucking* snap out of it, that would be great," prompted the blonde woman.

I stood there stunned for a moment longer, before finally turning my attention to Mateo. I searched his pockets and found a set of keys. I approached the woman and stood in front of her. Looking directly at me, she reached out, gesturing for the key ring. I handed it to her, and she immediately started looking for the right key. In under a minute, she unlocked herself and started helping the other women. I assisted the others in getting up and moving away from the soiled mattresses and buckets they were forced to use as toilets.

We huddled against the distant wall, close to Mateo's lifeless form. Too close for my comfort. And I still hadn't spoken a word as I stood face-to-face with the woman who had sought my help.

"You must be Desiree's replacement. I'm Katrina," she said.

I cleared my throat. "I'm Megan."

"Nice to meet you, Megan. Let's move Mateo and then figure out how the hell we're going to get out of here."

CHAPTER TWENTY-NINE

Michelle

"Where are they?" I asked, as I leaned forward in my seat, trying to catch a glimpse of them through the front window.

Perez said something to the taxi driver in Spanish that I didn't understand, and the driver pushed the car as fast as possible through the crowded city. We scoured every side street and alley, searching for the white van with tinted windows. The cab raced through the streets until we eventually reached an almost deserted highway.

"I think we either missed them or they went in the other direction," said Perez.

The disappointment was overwhelming. How would I ever find Megan now?

"We have to do something," I stressed, my eyes pleading with him to help me find my daughter.

"I know. We'll find her. Don't worry."

Don't worry? I couldn't do anything else. I discovered my daughter had been taken off the ship, where I had known she had been all along. But no one would listen to me when I repeatedly tried to convince everyone that she was still on the ship. Now I realized why Rochelle had put so much effort into discouraging me from believing that theory. She knew all along where Megan was. How could she do such a thing to me? To Megan? I was still struggling to come to terms with the reality that my best friend was behind this horrifying nightmare.

"I think we should call the police. Or the FBI. We can tell them—" Perez's phone suddenly rang, cutting me off.

He pulled the phone out of his pocket and glanced at the screen. "Perfect timing. It's the FBI agent working on Megan's case."

I moved in closer to Perez, eagerly listening to his end of the conversation. I wished he had used the speakerphone. I attempted to gesture to him to turn on the feature, but he was too engrossed in the conversation to pay attention.

"Perez here. Yes, agent. Listen, we think we saw Megan being taken off the ship this morning, but we've lost them and—what? That can't be accurate. Are you certain? But I don't see how that's possible. Can you just send an agent here to assist us in locating the van we saw earlier this morning?"

He paused briefly, attentively listening to the agent on the opposite side of the phone, as I anxiously awaited to be told what was being discussed.

"Yes, I understand. Yes, I am with Ms. Hamilton now, and I'll relay the news."

He ended the call, averting his gaze for a moment. I sensed that something was terribly wrong. Something he was reluctant to share with me. He instructed the cab driver to stop on the side of the highway. We pulled over on the dirt shoulder and he directed his attention toward me.

"I'm sorry, Michelle. The dental records of the traffic accident victim are a match for Megan. The FBI is confirming that she was killed in the accident in Playa del Carmen. Based on that, they no longer consider this an open investigation. I'm so sorry," he apologized, eyes lowered.

I was numb, unable to fully grasp the meaning of his words. The only thing I could say was a firm "no." It wasn't true. Megan was in a white van, being driven away from the ship. I shook my head.

"No, Captain. They're wrong. You know they are. I know what I saw this morning. And I'm sure of what Rochelle and Nate said too. Officer Cortez was taking someone off that ship who was heavily disguised. Why? What reason could he possibly have to do that? Who else could it be besides Megan? And why would he put a handicapped woman in a van and let her wheelchair just roll off? I'll tell you why. Because she isn't handicapped—she was drugged. I mean, this just all makes sense. It stands to reason that Rochelle would need crew members on her payroll to pull off kidnapping women from your cruise ships."

"Michelle, I understand this is terrifically challenging to comprehend. Particularly because we believe we have possibly found Megan. But according to the FBI, the dental records prove that it's her. Plus, her purse and ID were recovered at the accident scene. That evidence is difficult to argue against. I know you and I believe otherwise, but the FBI won't help us now. As far as they are concerned, your daughter has been positively identified as the car accident victim."

Seeing the pity on his face simply fueled my anger further. "Captain, I heard Nate tell Rochelle that their police contact and the medical examiner had both been paid. Why else would they bribe them? To say that was my daughter lying at the bottom of that ravine. That's why. To get me off the trail and force me to accept that she was gone so they could continue with their plans. The FBI will see that once they do their own dental exam. Maybe if they knew about all the cruises Rochelle and Nate have been on together, it might get their attention. But right now, I understand they are relying on the word of the medical examiner here in Mexico. But there's one quick way to prove that was Cortez and Megan this morning. Call the ship and have them bring Officer Cortez in. He won't be there. Because he's transporting my daughter!"

My voice grew louder and louder with each word until I was practically screaming at him. The driver's nervous glance met mine in the rearview mirror. Without saying a word, Perez unlocked his phone and began searching through his contacts.

"This is Perez. I need you to find Cortez and escort him to the office. If you're unable to locate him, issue a security announcement instructing him to report to station three immediately. I also need you to please examine today's sea card scan report and establish whether he used his card or employee ID to disembark from the ship. Also, please check if a passenger named Megan Hamilton was scanned as departing this morning. Or if any other sea card anomaly shows up on the report, notify me. Yes, get back to me as soon as possible. I'm off the ship, but have my cell on. Thank you."

I let out a sigh, feeling relieved. "Thank you, Captain."

Perez instructed the taxi driver to turn around, and we veered off in the opposite direction. We once again drove through Playa del Carmen and emerged on the other side with the sea on our left and jungle on our right. The highway gradually changed its course away from the ocean, and we moved inland, where we rode in silence until his cellphone rang twenty minutes later.

"Perez," he answered and then activated the speaker.

"Captain? It's Connelly. We were unable to locate Cortez, and he has not responded to our request to call in or report to station three. I checked the report for today, and his sea card was scanned as exiting at 9:58 a.m. this morning. There was no scan conducted for a passenger named Megan Hamilton. In fact, her sea card has shown zero activity over the last fifty-some hours. But I did find something else unusual."

"What was that?" asked Perez, glancing at me.

"The system highlighted a scan around the same time that Cortez exited, at 9:59 a.m. this morning, at the same exit location and gate, for a passenger named Desiree Fitzpatrick."

"Okay. What's the problem with that?"

"That passenger was on our cruise to Ensenada two weeks ago. The last activity on her card indicated she exited the ship upon arrival at the port of Los Angeles. As usual, her card was deactivated when she disembarked at our home port when the trip concluded. However, someone reactivated her sea card again yesterday and used it to leave the ship this morning."

"Are you certain of that?" asked Perez.

"Yes, sir. I verified it twice and had Stern check it too because it was so unusual."

"Thank you, Connelly. Let me know if Cortez reports in."

"Will do, Captain."

A feeling of triumph surged through me. I'd been proven right.

"So now do you believe me, Captain?"

"I am definitely convinced that something strange is going on, Ms. Hamilton. Only security personnel have the authority to deactivate or reactivate a sea card. It's puzzling why this other passenger's card was used this morning."

"I have an idea why. They can't very well use Megan's card and still have us believe she is lying dead in the morgue in Playa del Carmen, now can they? They need to make sure no one can dispute that. Using her sea card to scan her off the ship three days after her supposed death would be a huge red flag."

"Yes, that's an excellent point."

I turned my gaze forward, contemplating the significance of this newfound information. I considered reaching out to the FBI, but would they believe our story? Or would they assume I was a grieving mother searching for alternative theories instead of accepting what they believed to be the truth? I was too deep in thought to notice Perez's quick turn to look out the back window. Startled by his shout to the driver, I snapped back to the present. Perez pointed ahead as the cab swiftly made a sharp U-turn, speeding in the opposite direction. A white van with dark tinted rear windows vanished behind a hill on the highway's horizon. I let out a loud gasp and held on tightly to Perez's arm. *Megan!*

CHAPTER THIRTY

Megan

It took three of us to drag Mateo over to one of the mattresses. My first instinct was to shackle him so he couldn't come after us. Then I remembered he was dead.

I killed him. I had actually taken another human being's life. I didn't have much time to focus on it at that moment though. We had to devise a plan to escape the house, evade or disable two armed guards, and from a remote location seemingly in the middle of nowhere, find our way to safety. However, I realized that once I unpacked and processed all my emotions over killing Mateo, it would be a long time, if ever, before I could come to terms with it and potentially forgive myself.

As the other girls restlessly milled around the basement, Katrina pulled me aside.

"So I assume they got you from a cruise like they did all of us?"

"Yeah. I was on the *Jewel of the Sea.* You were all taken from cruise ships?"

"Yep. The same ship as yours. Well, I think so, anyway. A couple of the girls were visiting from Italy and their English is kind of hard to understand sometimes. But as far as we can tell between the language challenges and a weird game of charades, we were all abducted off the *Jewel of the Sea* while cruising to Mexico."

"But how? How are they getting away with this without someone noticing the pattern of missing women? That's crazy!"

"Well, I went on a singles cruise alone, and a couple of the girls don't have family or anyone who would even realize they were missing for a few weeks. Their friends might just think they were busy when they got back or whatever. I really don't know how they choose their victims. But Nicole – that's her over there in the blue – she speaks Spanish and heard Mateo and our kidnapper, Nate, talking about it. They scan our cruise cards when the ships dock back in LA. So if anyone were to investigate, it would look like we got off the ship as planned and then just disappeared into LA. Not a bad idea when you think about it."

"Oh, my God. Rochelle has this all figured out."

"Who?"

"Rochelle Kendrick. She's the mastermind behind all of this."

"How do you know who the boss is? And seriously, it's a woman who runs this?"

"Yes. She's my mother's best friend."

"What? Are you serious?"

"I didn't know any of this until Nate took me. And my mom knows nothing about it. It was a complete shock, believe me. We both trusted her unconditionally. Nate told me they had to take me to replace another girl who had an accident. I assume that's Desiree, the woman you mentioned before?"

"Yes. But Desiree didn't have an accident. They killed her. She needed her insulin. She told them over and over, but they did nothing to help her. They might as well have shot her. It would have been more humane than the way she suffered. It took her a week to die, and there was nothing we could do to help her. The bastards," she cursed, glaring at Mateo's limp body.

"I'm sorry you had to go through that. But I plan on getting out of here. And when I do, I am going to make sure that Rochelle, Nate, and anyone else involved in this gets what they deserve."

"I'm sure I speak for the rest of the girls when I say we'll do whatever it takes to make that happen. Now that they have brought you here, it won't be long until the buyers show up. They were stupid enough to discuss their plans in front of us whenever they brought in food and stuff. I guess they didn't realize Nicole understood them, or they didn't care, thinking we would never get away, so what did it matter?"

"I saw two armed guards with rifles when we drove in. Maybe assault rifles. I really don't know for sure. I didn't see any other vehicles or guards. At first I thought there had to be more guards, but since they had you chained up down here, they probably didn't think they needed any more. That's definitely a plus for us."

"Yeah. We outnumber them, for sure. Plus, now we have a gun," she said, glancing down at the weapon in my hand. "We've only ever seen Mateo and one other guy in here, presumably one of the guards you saw, as he always had a rifle with him."

The good news was there were ten of us and likely only two of them, and if we could disarm them and seize their guns, that would give us a total of three weapons for protection. The bad news was the ten of us were dressed in cocktail dresses and high heels, resembling recent apocalypse survivors. Not exactly ideal for hiking through what appeared to be wild jungle. I reminded myself to take things one step at a time. Our first priority was to devise a plot to deal with the guards before Nate, Rochelle, our buyers, or any other potential threats arrived.

We desperately needed to come up with a plan. I had nothing solid. Besides attempting to overpower the guards or escaping unnoticed, I wasn't sure what to do, and both options had major drawbacks. However, all the women were wearing spiked heels, and mine had proven to be a useful weapon. If necessary, the unarmed women could use theirs for protection. It wasn't an ideal strategy, especially against two armed guards. It was as futile as bringing a knife to a gunfight. But we had no other option than to work with what we had. Katrina signaled the others to come over, as if she could read my thoughts. We stood in a circle, everyone's gaze fixed on Katrina, who had assumed the role of group leader. I was fine with that. I felt I had no useful contribution to make other than to point out how totally screwed we were.

"So I think the best thing to do is distract the guards and take them out so we can get their guns," said Katrina.

"Take them out?" I asked.

"Yes. We won't kill them if we don't have to, but if it comes down to them or me, I know where I stand. They're selling us as sex slaves to some freak. I don't know about the rest of you, but I'm not gonna let that happen now that we have half a friggin' chance to survive this."

I nodded along with the rest of the women, as a few murmured their agreement with Katrina. She raised a valid argument. It might come down to us or them. Killing Mateo had left me shaken to my core. But as bad as I felt about taking a life, I also wasn't willing to jeopardize my own in return. These people were criminals with no regard for us. Plain and simple.

"I have a plan," offered Katrina, glancing around the group.

Silence fell around the room as Katrina shared her idea. While it wasn't entirely foolproof, it just might work. We planned to lure both guards to a single location by firing the pistol I had confiscated from Mateo. Once they were together, we would eliminate one of them by shooting then disarming him, while the rest of us charged the other guard from behind. It was a solid plan considering our circumstances, and our advantage in numbers increased our chances of success. Either we would be armed and on our way to freedom or we would face a disastrous outcome if it went wrong.

We finalized our plan, with everyone assigned their respective roles. I just hoped that the two foreigners in our group understood what was happening. Although they seemed to, Katrina was right in stating that English was clearly not their first language. Despite that, I was so close to believing we could succeed. Right up until the moment we heard footsteps approaching the basement door, that is.

As my eyes locked on Katrina's, a sinking sensation filled my heart, fully understanding the gravity of our situation. This wasn't what we had planned. We were about to encounter the enemy face-to-face, and we were caught completely off guard.

CHAPTER THIRTY-ONE

Michelle

"Is that them? Is that the van that has Megan?" I asked, leaning between the seats to get a better look.

"It sure looked like it to me," said Perez.

He spoke to the driver in a rush, gesturing ahead to the van in the distance. As the driver pressed the accelerator to the floor, the taxi surged ahead, slamming me against the back seat. In a matter of minutes, we pulled alongside the van, our driver honking the horn continuously. Perez gestured for the van driver to pull over. Glancing in our direction, the man frowned and shook his head while motioning to us to move on. The van pulled ahead of us and Perez barked directions to our driver, who sped up again. Perez reached into his back pocket and flipped open his security badge, pressing it against the back window. The van driver's eyes grew wide, and he slowed down. Our taxi kept pace with him as Perez once again signaled for him to pull over. This time, he guided the van onto the shoulder of the highway and came to a stop. Without waiting for the taxi to fully stop, we swiftly exited the car.

I ran to the passenger side of the van, pounding on the side doors as I passed them, while Perez went to the driver's door. He yanked it open and began speaking rapid Spanish to the driver. The man looked terrified. I didn't know what the captain was saying to him, but the man's response was a series of shrugs and head shakes. I pulled the passenger door open and hoisted myself onto the seat. I stretched over the bucket seat to peer into the back of the van.

"Megan!" I yelled.

The van was empty. My stomach did a flip as I realized we were too late. He had already delivered her. I impulsively lunged at the driver before I could restrain myself. "Where is my daughter?" I screamed at him.

He swatted my hands away and produced a gun from the back of his waistband. I scrambled back into the passenger seat, raising my hands in surrender. But he wasn't paying attention to me. The gun was pointed at Perez, who was backing away from the van slowly with his hands held high. I reached for the door handle and cautiously made my way out of the van. The last thing I wanted was to be taken by this man and separated from Perez. I would be of no help to Megan if that happened.

Perez spoke calmly to the man, who then jumped out of the driver's seat. Waving the gun erratically, he shouted at Perez and our cab driver. I didn't know what he was saying, but judging by his actions, I assumed he was trying to make a getaway. I snuck around the back of the van and stole a glimpse just as the gunman climbed into the front passenger seat of the taxi. He leveled the gun at the driver, coercing him to drive off. As the taxi sped away, it left us in a cloud of dust.

"No!" I screamed after them. "How will we find Megan now?"

Sobbing, I buried my face in my hands as I leaned against the van. I didn't notice Perez getting into the van. The engine roared to life, and I got up and sprinted to the driver's door.

"He left the keys!" I cried, excitedly.

I hurried to the passenger side and quickly got in the seat, where I fastened my seatbelt and turned to Perez. "Let's go, we're going to lose him."

Despite my frustration, he kept tinkering with the dashboard GPS, completely ignoring me. We needed to catch up to the van driver in the taxi, the one person within our reach who knew Megan's whereabouts, and stop wasting precious time. While Nate and Rochelle were aware of where she was taken, I had no doubt that they would be uncooperative or simply deny everything.

"Captain, we need to go. Please, he is our only link to my daughter right now," I pleaded.

"That's not true. We have an even better option. The GPS is set to a remote location approximately twenty-five miles from here. It's in the same direction he came from. I believe this GPS could lead us directly to your daughter," he responded, glancing in my direction.

Could it really be that simple? Were we on the verge of rescuing Megan?

"So what are we waiting for, then?"

"I have no idea who else is at that address. We need to exercise caution. Arriving in their van without their driver is out of the question. That would immediately raise a ton of red flags with them. Ideally, we could ask the authorities for their help, but given the FBI's recent call to me, I'm certain they would be no help."

"No way. The FBI has already absolved themselves of any responsibility. And we know Rochelle paid off someone in both the police department and the medical examiner's office. I don't trust the police in Playa del Carmen now. Do you?"

"Not really, no. Until we determine who is accepting bribes, we really can't trust anyone. But I don't think it's a wise decision to just go barging in on whoever is at this house. They are most likely armed. I think the smartest thing to do is to keep the house under surveillance and gather intelligence."

I knew he was right, but I felt an overwhelming urge to storm the place and rescue my daughter. I quickly realized that we likely had only one opportunity to rescue her. With no assistance from the police and the FBI refusing involvement, we had to use our wits. Whoever was at that house didn't yet suspect we were onto them. That provided us with a significant advantage.

"Ready?" Perez asked me.

"Ready as I'll ever be. Thank you for believing me and sticking with me to find Megan. It means everything to me. She would be lost to me forever if not for your help."

"Well, I have to confess I didn't believe you at first. And I thought you might have been mistaken about her being taken off the ship this morning. I was obviously wrong, and I apologize."

"I can't say I really blame you. This entire thing is so unbelievable. I'm just glad you humored me."

He nodded and put the van in gear. "Me too. Hold on, I'm going to get us there in record time."

I tightened my grip on the center console as he maneuvered the vehicle around, tires screeching on the pavement. We raced forward in the van, heading toward Megan's rescue.

CHAPTER THIRTY-TWO

Megan

For a brief moment, I couldn't remember how to breathe as I listened to the footsteps on the floor above us. No one moved, completely transfixed. Katrina recovered from her daze first.

"Everyone back in place, quick!" she whispered. "Put the shackles around your feet, but don't snap them in place. Stand that mattress up to cover Mateo's body. Until we know who is up there, we have to play along. If it's just one of the guards bringing food and water, then we can surprise him when he gets close. Megan, give me the gun," she prompted, reaching out to me.

I was more than happy to turn the firearm over to her. I had never pulled the trigger of a gun before. The only thing I knew for sure was to aim and shoot. Did it have a safety? Did I need to slide the rack back? I saw that once in a movie, where a woman was learning to shoot for self-defense. I doubted my target would be standing still, and I had no clue what I was doing. Evidently, Katrina had some experience with guns because she handled it like a seasoned pro.

We hurriedly returned to the chains and mattresses, sliding our ankles into the shackles. I positioned myself against the mattress that concealed Mateo's body and attempted to appear like everything was normal. The basement door creaked open, and a voice called out down the stairs.

"*Mateo! Por qué estás tardando tanto?*"

"He wants to know what's taking him so long down here," whispered Nicole.

"Tell him Mateo brought the new girl and left, but we need some water," said Katrina.

"*Èl no está aquí abajo. Trajo a la chica nueva y se fue. Necesitamos agua,*" shouted Nicole.

"*Siempre necesitas algo. Solo un momento,*" he shouted back.

"He says just a minute. What are you going to do?" asked Nicole.

"Everyone just act normal. I'm going to knock him out and then shackle him down here. That will hopefully only leave one guard to deal with."

Scruffy boots emerged on the stairs as footsteps echoed across the basement. The guard came into full view in a matter of seconds. My pulse quickened because I was positive he sensed something was off. But he seemed oblivious and paid no attention to any of us as he continued forward with a pitcher, presumably containing the water Nicole requested.

Before he could get to Nicole, Katrina reached out for the pitcher and coughed, her hair hanging limply over most of her face. I had to give her credit. She played her part well because she looked pitiful and harmless. The guard changed direction and leaned down to place the pitcher on the floor in front of her. In a sudden movement that took the guard by surprise, Katrina sprung up and forcefully brought the gun hidden behind her back down onto his head. While it didn't quite knock him out, it had enough impact to stun him. He took a few unsteady steps before getting tangled in Nicole's shackles and landing in a heap on the ground. While he was still dazed, Katrina and Nicole tackled him and swiftly removed the rifle strap from his shoulder. I rushed over to them and snatched the rifle, making sure the guard couldn't reach it. The others helped pin him down as he fought to get free. In just seconds, both of his ankles were chained. He yelled angrily and spat at us while he tried to get out of the chains. I didn't need to be fluent in Spanish to pick up on some of the curse words he shouted at us.

"Callarse la boca!" Nicole shouted at him.

He paused his yelling, glaring at her.

"Okay. That's better," said Katrina. "Tell him he has two choices. He ends up like Mateo or he answers our questions, and stops yelling."

Nicole acted as Katrina's translator, while the guard eyed her suspiciously.

"Vete a la mierda, perra. Vienen por ti."

Everyone's gaze was on Nicole, eager to hear what he had shared with her.

"He basically told me to fuck off, that they were coming for us."

Walking to the dark corner of the basement, Katrina grabbed one end of the propped-up mattress and flipped it over. Mateo was lying on his side with the shoe heel imbedded deeply into his temple, just as we had left him. Dried blood marked a path down his face and neck, and one of his legs was bent at an unnatural angle. It made me physically ill to know that I had done that to him, but I pushed the thought away and refocused on the guard.

The sight of Mateo made the guard's eyes widen, and he swallowed nervously. Katrina approached him, stopping mere inches from him and aiming the gun at his head. She looked directly at him as she spoke.

"Tell him I want to know how many more guards are here and when someone else is expected to arrive. Are they taking us to the buyers, or will the buyers come here to get us? Tell him he has one opportunity to talk and then I'm going to shoot him. Or maybe I'll save the bullet and just put a heel in his head like his friend over there," she pressed, nodding her head toward Mateo's lifeless body.

"If he tells us what we want to know, we'll let him live. He can explain to his bosses how he and Mateo let a bunch of women get the jump on both of them and escape."

With a nod, Nicole rapidly translated Katrina's message to the guard. He glanced over at Mateo nervously. As Nicole asked questions, he spoke rapidly and nodded.

"He says it is just him, one other guard, and Mateo here. The only other person who comes is the driver, but he's gone now. No one else is ever here until the buyers send their runners to get us. At least, that's how it usually goes. Now that all of us are here and Desiree has been replaced, the runners will be here tonight. He says he doesn't know what time, but they always come at night."

"Okay, so we need to figure out what to do, and fast. Are there any vehicles here? A phone? Where is the closest town?" asked Katrina.

Following a short discussion with the guard, Nicole shifted her focus back to Katrina.

"There are no vehicles here and no phones. The driver brings supplies. He says the nearest town is back toward Playa del Carmen, southwest of here. A small town with only a few houses and businesses. But there are other houses on the way there. There is nothing but rain forest for miles in the other direction. He says we should just kill him because the bosses are going to, anyway. If we shoot him, it will be more merciful than what they will do to him."

"Merciful, huh? Like he and Mateo were to us when they kept us chained up down here? As merciful as they were when they let Desiree die a slow and painful death? No. He doesn't deserve mercy. He deserves whatever they dish out. It's out of our hands. Let them take care of him. Our only responsibility is to ourselves and each other. Come on, girls. Let's go see if there is anything in this house that we can use to get out of here."

While Katrina aimed her gun at the guard, Nicole tied his hands with his belt and gagged him with an old rag. Once he was restrained, the group walked past while I stole a final glimpse at him. Several women expressed their contempt by spitting at him, and I understood their anger. We paid no attention to his muffled begging for a quick death as we made our way up the basement stairs.

CHAPTER THIRTY-THREE

Michelle

As we raced by the sparsely populated terrain, I stared out of the van's window. The hills were speckled with scattered houses, barely visible through the thick trees and vegetation, yet we came across no cities and encountered minimal traffic. The overwhelming desolation made the thought of facing an emergency or car trouble in the area seem daunting, and it was clear why Rochelle picked this area for a staging house. Every time I thought about her being the mastermind behind a trafficking ring, it made me feel ill. I just couldn't fathom that there were no signs that something was off with her. For two decades, she was my closest friend. Looking back, I thought she just had a genuine passion for going on cruises. But the more I thought about it, the more peculiar it was that we never drove to the port or boarded the ships together. Without fail, she would always come up with a rational reason for us to meet on board. It all made sense now. She had to handle her business affairs with Nate and any assisting crew members. I felt like a complete idiot, and I would carry the burden of my naïveté forever if anything happened to Megan.

Perez spoke up, as if he could read the thoughts inside my head. "You can't blame yourself for this, you know. Your friend is a criminal. It was her, not you, who did this. She is unquestionably adept at disguising her true character."

"Captain, I've known and been close friends with Rochelle for twenty years. It's obvious that I was incredibly gullible to not see that something wasn't right with her."

"Antonio. Please call me Antonio. And I disagree with you. I dismissed her as having any involvement. The blame falls on me, if anyone. I completely neglected my duty to fully investigate her and Nate, and it was ignorant and unprofessional of me not to do so. I have to admit, for a short time, I had suspicions you were involved in your daughter's disappearance, and I am ashamed to say that now."

"You thought I had a role in Megan's disappearance?" I asked, shocked to hear that from him.

"I had to consider it, yes. You'd be amazed at how frequently a family member is directly involved or has information they don't disclose in a loved one's disappearance. Before I joined the cruise line, I was a homicide detective in San Jose. So I have extensive experience in investigating missing persons cases. I honestly thought Megan would turn up the next day, having recovered from her hangover and spending the night with someone she met on the ship. It's a common occurrence with the younger crowd on cruise ships."

"I tried to tell you. That's not Megan's nature. She is excessively careful. She would never engage is such high-risk behavior."

"I realize that now, and I'm sorry. I will do everything in my power to get her back. I give you my word."

I acknowledged with a nod, then returned my gaze to the scenery outside. Regardless of his efforts to help me get Megan back, I couldn't shake off a hint of resentment that our current predicament could have been avoided if only he had listened to me two days ago. But it felt pointless to blame myself or Antonio for it. My focus had to be on the current situation. Besides, he was right in saying that Rochelle was entirely to blame. The responsibility for Megan's abduction rested squarely on her shoulders.

We approached the GPS destination shortly after. Antonio slowed the van as we drove past the house. The single-story house, set back from the highway on a long dirt driveway, had a neighboring building that was too small to serve as a garage. There were no vehicles in sight.

"It looks deserted. We can't be too late. We came straight here. And the driver must have just dropped her off, right? He didn't have time to do much else. From the time he left the ship to the time we intercepted him, he couldn't have gone anywhere else," I mused.

"Yes. I suspect their intention is to make it appear as if nobody is there. I'll park a little farther up the highway, behind that outcropping of rocks up ahead. We can walk back down and take cover behind that hill," he suggested, gesturing toward a hill covered in dense patches of brush and several trees.

I wanted to ram the van straight into the house's front door and grab Megan. But I had no way of knowing for sure that she was even in there. I prayed she was. She had to be. Because if she wasn't, then we would have no other leads to pursue. That meant returning to the ship and attempting to extract information from Rochelle and Nate. And I knew that would be a long shot.

Antonio pulled the van off the road and parked behind a large boulder to conceal it from the highway. We exited at once and made our way a few hundred feet back to the hill, which provided a vantage point of the house. We got comfortable, laying on our stomachs, watching the house.

Antonio checked his watch regularly. I knew we would have to return to the ship by late afternoon for the cruise home. Well, Antonio would need to go back. There was no way I was going back to Los Angeles without my daughter. And neither was Rochelle. I would use any means, including dragging her by her hair, to get her off that ship if I had to. But one way or another, I was going to track down my daughter today. Going back to the ship together would be much easier if she were in that house. From there, Antonio would then decide how to handle Rochelle and Nate. I had no choice but to leave it up to him. But if I had my way, once Megan was found, both Rochelle and Nate would be tossed overboard into the open sea as shark bait.

CHAPTER THIRTY-FOUR

Megan

Katrina cautiously peered out from behind the basement door and motioned for us to follow her. The house was deathly quiet. I couldn't decide if the silence was a relief or not, as the stillness was both eerie and unsettling.

We crept out of the basement and straight into a tiny kitchen. It was crowded with all ten of us inside, making it difficult to move. I looked through the top window of the back door and saw no one outside. At least not at that immediate moment.

To keep quiet, the women removed their shoes and we moved from the kitchen into a small living room. The couch, worn and tattered, was pushed against the wall facing the front door. The coffee table was littered with empty beer bottles, overflowing ashtrays, and half-eaten food containers, some still in the plastic carryout bags. Resting on a plastic crate in the corner was a small television with a rabbit ear antenna, the only other furniture in the room. There was a hallway to the left, with doors on either side. When Katrina glanced back at me, I raised my eyebrows in response. To ensure we were alone in the house and look for potential weapons, we had to search the rooms. Two guns and ten women left us lacking eight weapons.

I tiptoed toward Katrina while keeping the rifle at my side. Signaling the others to stay, she motioned for me to follow, her gun raised and prepared to fire. My heart was beating so fast I was convinced anyone within a foot of me would be able to hear it. I wasn't sure I was the right person to help Katrina search the house, but I suppose she chose me because I had the only other gun. Or maybe it was because I took out Mateo earlier. I wondered what she would think of me if she knew what I had done to escape the guard back on the ship, that I was to blame for his death too? I certainly wasn't going to mention it. I guess, compared to everyone else, I was the most composed. Which was a terrifying thought, as I was literally on the verge of a panic attack, and even the smallest thing would probably send me running back to the living room, screaming in fear. Coming to a standstill in front of the first door, Katrina turned around to give me a look.

"On three," she whispered to me.

Who was this woman? A covert CIA agent? I could barely hold myself upright and she was leading a tactical raid on the bedrooms. Holding up three fingers, she began counting down to one, then opened the door quietly and stepped inside. I raised the rifle to shoulder level, mimicking what I had seen in movies, although there was a very real danger of me accidentally shooting Katrina in the back with my trembling finger poised over the trigger. Despite my nerves, I followed her into the room. Much of the space was taken up by a double bed and a chest of drawers. A door to the left was slightly ajar, and Katrina used her gun to pull it open. Apart from a few men's shirts on wire hangers, it was empty. It was too small for anyone to conceal themselves in, so I breathed a sigh of relief.

Back in the hall, we went through the same procedure again, this time in another bedroom and the bathroom. Just like the first bedroom, the second one had a double bed and dresser, but the room was larger. There were multiple suitcases in the closet, all stacked on top of each other.

We made our way back to the living room, where Katrina ensured our safety by locking us inside and using the deadbolt on the front door. She signaled for the others to follow us to the bigger bedroom at the end of the hallway. Once inside, she locked the door and took a seat on the bed.

"There are some suitcases in the closet. Let's look through them and see if there is anything we can change into. It might get cold here at night and we are going to be on foot. Try to get some boots or sturdy sneakers," she said.

The women started removing the luggage from the closet, and one by one, they each grabbed a suitcase. After a couple of minutes, they realized the luggage belonged to them.

"That kind of makes sense, actually," said Katrina. "They have to get rid of our luggage when we dock in Los Angeles to make it look like we got off the ship. If housekeeping found all our things in our cabins, that would raise some red flags."

"Why not just dump it then?" I asked.

"Well, they either didn't want to take a chance of anything ever being found, or more likely, they bring stuff back for their wives and girlfriends to go through."

"Well, they aren't getting my Chanel dress. Or my Louboutin shoes," grumbled one of the girls.

"Sorry, but you're not going to be able to carry extra clothing or shoes through the jungle. Nothing in our luggage is worth taking that risk for. It's just stuff. Nothing is so important that we need to take it with us. Just hurry up, everyone. Get changed and let's find some containers to bring water with us. We need to get out of here before the buyers arrive," urged Katrina, rummaging through one of the suitcases.

"My suitcase isn't here," I said, looking around.

"Here, you can wear something of mine. We're about the same size," offered Nicole.

She tossed me a complete outfit—jeans, t-shirt, hoodie, socks, baseball cap, and sneakers. Finally getting out of the uncomfortable, scratchy sequined dress was such a relief. And I was grateful for her spare shoes. The sneakers were a little tight, but they would do. Wearing those heels again was entirely out of the question for me. Mainly because one of them was still lodged in Mateo's head.

In less than ten minutes, we were changed and returned to the small kitchen. While searching the cupboards for anything we could use as makeshift water carriers, one of the girls opened the refrigerator and let out a squeal of delight. She reached her hand inside and held up a bottle of water. The bottom shelf was packed with water bottles. I hurried to the living room and snatched a few of the plastic bags that held the half-eaten food containers in them. After filling them with the water bottles, we were all set to leave.

Of course, we still faced the problem of the second guard. Since we had heard no noise outside, I held onto hope that just one guard remained. We returned to the living room to brainstorm our next move. We tried to peek out the front windows, but the curtains obstructed our view and we hesitated to move them for fear of being noticed. We debated on whether to go for a full-scale attack by charging the guard or to bide our time and wait for him to enter. Both plans had major flaws. If there were multiple guards, the situation could become disastrous, particularly since most of us lacked experience with firearms. Out of all of us, Katrina was the only one with experience firing a weapon. On the flip side, if we waited for the guard to enter, it might be too late by then. Without knowing when the buyers would arrive, if the guard remained on patrol, it would merely increase their numbers against us. It was almost certain that they would have the upper hand and overpower us.

As we were in the process of deliberating, fate stepped in and decided for us. The front doorknob rattled as someone attempted to open the door, and the sound of a man's muffled voice came from behind the door. We looked at Nicole for translation.

"He wants the other guard to open the door. He's asking why it's locked," she whispered.

"We can't let him think anything is wrong. If he has a radio or a cell, he could call and let them know he needs help," Katrina whispered back.

While some of the women were directed into the kitchen, Nicole, Katrina, another woman, and I remained in the living room. Katrina reached out to unlock the deadbolt and swiftly took cover behind the door. Nicole and the other woman stood in the corner of the hall, out of view, while I stood beside Katrina.

I held my breath as I watched the door open slowly and sunlight flood the dim room.

CHAPTER THIRTY-FIVE

Megan

Everything happened in such a blur that fear never had a chance to set in. Katrina brought the gun down on the guard's head the moment he stepped inside the house. Just like the other guard, it didn't render him unconscious, but it startled him enough to disorient him. Struggling to maintain his balance, he stumbled into the room, knocking over the crate that held the small TV as Katrina rushed to stand before him, her gun aimed at his head, while I grabbed his rifle and tossed it to Nicole. I slammed the front door shut and secured it with the deadbolt.

He straightened up, his attention shifting to me, where I held my rifle pointed in his direction. Concealing my trembling, I kept the rifle butt against my shoulder, hoping he wouldn't notice how scared I was. The defeat in his expression made it clear that he recognized the rifle as belonging to the other guard. Katrina gestured for him to sit on the couch while he raised his hands in surrender.

Nicole hurried over to join us after she received a nod from Katrina.

"Ask him about other guards and if there is a vehicle here."

Nicole confronted the guard, who smirked and ignored her.

Taking a step forward, Katrina racked the slide on the gun. She held the weapon to his temple as I moved in closer and aimed my rifle at his head.

"Tell him unless he gives us information, he is no use to us."

Nicole put on her game face as she carefully translated Katrina's words. The guard glanced at Nicole, then Katrina, and finally at me. I responded by tightening my grip on the rifle.

Fear registered in the guard's eyes as he spoke rapidly to Nicole. I could almost feel sorry for him if he hadn't planned to deliver us to strangers as sex slaves. Nicole posed questions, and for a solid five minutes, he provided answers. Having gathered the information she wanted, she then directed her attention to us.

"He says there is no vehicle here. He said the same thing the other guy did. That the driver in the van brings supplies once a week and drops off girls. Then buyers come to get them. They get to go home every two weeks, when there are no deliveries. They work two weeks on and two weeks off. We are their last shipment for the next two weeks. He doesn't know what time the buyers will come, but it's always after dark. I think he's telling the truth. His story matches with the other guard."

"Okay, let's get him down to the basement and chain him up with the other guy. Then we can look around outside and make sure it's safe to take off," said Katrina.

Nicole directed the guard to stand, making it clear to him that if he tried anything, he would be shot without warning. While he descended the basement stairs, we maintained a few steps of distance behind him. He reached the bottom step, where he was confronted with the sight of the other guard chained to the wall and Mateo's lifeless body in the corner. He turned back to us to plead for his life, but it fell on deaf ears. There was absolutely no chance we were going to allow him to remain free. We guided him to the opposite end of the room, ensuring he was out of reach of the other guard. I kept my rifle trained on him while Katrina secured the shackles. We turned to leave, but before I walked away, I grabbed a water bottle from my bag and tossed one to each of them. I wasn't a monster. No matter what they had done to us, I couldn't lower myself to their level and leave them with no water. I was certain that whoever arrived to pick us up tonight would discover them. But would they set them free? I didn't know. I wasn't sure about the criminal code when permitting your prisoners to escape. But I did what I could, because the bodies were piling up, and I honestly didn't think I could handle the burden of yet another death weighing on my conscience.

We climbed the stairs to the living room, where the other women waited anxiously for us. It was time to venture outside and make sure we were alone. Katrina tucked her long hair into her beanie and zipped up her lightweight jacket. I pulled my baseball cap down to cover my forehead and took a deep, calming breath. I felt my heart thumping as Katrina swung open the front door and I trailed behind her onto the porch. The warm afternoon sun was shining brightly, and I regretted wearing Nicole's hoodie. There was complete stillness except for the trill of birds. We stepped off the porch and silently circled the house. We didn't encounter anyone, but I remained on guard for a surprise attack. I kept waiting for someone to jump out and charge at us. There was a small outbuilding several hundred feet from the house, and as much as I did not want to go in there, I knew we had no choice. Katrina gestured for me to remain on one side of the door while she was positioned on the opposite side. Once again, she counted down from three and then burst through the door.

Inside were various tools and an old, rusty toolbox that had seen better days. At least we could use some of the tools as weapons if needed. We rounded up a small collection of hammers, screw drivers, and gardening tools for the other women and headed back to the house through the back door. As a group, we decided to head toward Playa del Carmen and look for the first house where we could borrow a phone. Our plan was to avoid the main highway, walking beside it to stay out of sight as much as possible. The identity and timing of our potential attackers were unknown, and we couldn't risk being noticed by the wrong people. It wouldn't be easy to hide ten women. Equipped with our three firearms and our other various improvised weapons, we left the house and ventured into the cover of the trees, leaving the property behind. We had a great vantage point of the highway, but there was plenty of vegetation and trees to provide cover if needed.

We trudged through the dense jungle, feeling the weight of the scorching heat. I had my hoodie wrapped around my waist while my hat failed to protect me from the constant swarm of bugs targeting my face. All of us were beat and overheated. Due to their insufficient calorie intake over the past week, none of the women had the energy required for the hike, leading to more frequent rest stops than I would have liked. Even after walking for an hour, we still hadn't spotted any other houses. Seeing glimpses of the highway kept us oriented in the right direction. We resumed our journey after one of our frequent rest breaks, and soon after, a house appeared in sight. Nicole pointed and let out a little cheer. With a fresh burst of energy, we set off in that direction.

We stopped at the edge of a gravel driveway in clear view of the highway. I felt exposed and vulnerable out in the open like that, because at that moment my greatest fear was being caught by the people who were coming to buy us. Ten women hiking in the forest would definitely grab their attention, and I estimated it would take them around two seconds to connect the dots. But the opportunity to find a phone to call the police or a vehicle to return to the ship was too strong, so we began making our way up the driveway toward the house.

CHAPTER THIRTY-SIX

Michelle

With each passing minute, I became more and more uncomfortable. As I lay on the hill, feeling the cold, hard ground beneath me, I was reminded of how at my age my body was no longer very tolerant of such discomfort. I moved around trying to find a more forgiving position, but it was useless. Running to catch the kidnappers this morning left my calf muscles feeling achy. I undoubtedly needed to get more exercise. I had a Pilates video at home that I had never even bothered to put in the DVD player, and I was paying for that now. I swatted at an ant crawling on my arm and wondered what other insects might be ready to strike. I was not an outdoorsy type. But I would endure lying here all night if it meant getting my daughter back.

"Are you alright? I can take my jacket off and you can use it as a cushion. Maybe that will be more comfortable," offered Antonio.

My restlessness must have given away my discomfort. "No, I'm fine. Just trying to get settled into a better position. There are tiny rocks in the dirt. I'm like the princess and the pea. I can feel every single one of them," I complained, glancing at him.

He smiled and nodded in agreement. Antonio had to be close to my age, so I was surprised he wasn't retired yet. Maybe he had a genuine passion for his job. I had heard that retiring can be challenging for many police officers after a career full of drama and excitement. I'd bet he wasn't so enamored with his job today, no thanks to me.

As we lay in silence for several minutes, we suddenly noticed that one of the guards was on the move. Another guard had entered the house earlier and had yet to return. If this guard followed suit, it could provide us with the opportunity to approach the house discreetly and get a better look. Making his way onto the porch, he tried to open the front door. When it didn't budge, he pounded on the door and shouted something. I looked at Antonio.

"I can't tell what he's saying. It's too far away," he said, shrugging.

After a minute, the front door opened a crack, and he looked like he stumbled inside or was pulled into the house. The door swung shut almost immediately. That was peculiar. Something was off about the way he entered the house, but I couldn't pinpoint what it was.

"That was weird. Did that look strange to you?" I asked Antonio.

"Yes. Almost like he was caught off guard when he entered the house. And the other guard has yet to come back to his post. That leaves no one protecting the house. That strikes me as odd. Until now, they have been very diligent in patrolling the area. I guess we will just have to be patient and see what happens."

After twenty minutes, the door finally opened again. Two figures emerged from the house, one wielding a handgun and another armed with a rifle. They surveyed the yard and conducted a search of the surrounding area, including the small shed next to the house. They exited the shed, each carrying a handful of tools. This was getting stranger by the minute. They looked like women to me, although it was tough to say for sure, from our distant vantage point on the hill, especially with their baseball cap, beanie, and oversized jackets. The jeans and shoes they wore appeared to be women's clothing. And something in the way they moved convinced me these were not men.

"Antonio, I think those are two women. I'm certain of it. What if the captives have somehow taken the guards prisoner?"

"It's so hard to tell from here, but something is definitely wrong. Let's be ready to move quickly if we need to."

I sat up and brushed the dirt off my shirt. Moments later, a group of ten emerged from the house and proceeded in single file toward the shelter of the trees, vanishing from our sight. Without a doubt, they were women. We could see that even from far away.

"Those are women! They're escaping!" I cried.

"Come on. Let's get back to the van and find them," said Antonio, grabbing my hand and pulling me up.

We raced back to the van and hurried inside. Antonio drove along the highway slowly as we both searched for the women. After driving up and down the highway for almost an hour without seeing them, I was getting frantic.

On another pass farther down the road, I finally spotted them darting between the trees and then up a gravel driveway toward a small bungalow.

"There!" I shouted, pointing.

To my surprise, Antonio wrenched the steering wheel, veering us off the road and into the grove of trees, missing the driveway altogether. Thankfully, the growth was sparse enough that we could make our way between the trees and back onto the gravel in pursuit of the women. Despite honking the horn repeatedly to grab their attention, they simply ran faster. They disappeared around the side of the house and further into the forest. I was terrified we would lose them, so when the trees became too dense and made it impassable, I hopped out of the van before it stopped and yelled Megan's name.

I paused and listened, but heard nothing in response. I screamed again. "Megan, stop! It's Mom!"

I recited a prayer under my breath that she was with them and had heard me. I knew deep down that if she wasn't part of this group, all hope of ever finding my daughter would be lost.

CHAPTER THIRTY-SEVEN

Megan

Just as we were halfway up the driveway, I heard a vehicle and looked back. A white van with dark tinted windows slowed down on the highway, honking its horn repeatedly. My heart sank, and we paused as I stared in disbelief. They had found us. It was the van that brought me here. We experienced a moment of fear-induced paralysis, followed by a rush of adrenaline. Then we ran as fast as our legs would carry us, around the house and further into the shelter of the trees. Throughout the entire time, the van kept blaring the horn. It had left the gravel drive and was now off the road, attempting to trail us into the rain forest. I stole a quick look over my shoulder while I was running. The van came to a halt, unable to move due to the dense clutter of trees. I picked up speed and crashed through the forest as the van doors opened. At any moment, I expected to feel a bullet tear through my back. Instead, I heard a woman call my name. I panicked, believing it was Rochelle.

Suddenly, a familiar voice screamed and echoed through the trees. I knew what I heard, but it didn't make any sense.

Mom?

"Megan! Stop! It's Mom!"

I stopped and turned, gasping for air, only to see my mom running down the driveway toward me at top speed, an unfamiliar man at her side.

"Katrina! Wait! That's my mother!" I yelled at her.

The women stopped and looked back to see what was happening. Standing motionless, I struggled to make sense of what was in front of me. I had no idea what was going on. What on earth was my mom doing here? Was she in the same van the people who had abducted me had used? And the man with her, wearing the *Jewel of the Sea* crew uniform. Who was he? Even though I was utterly confused, I didn't hesitate to rush to my mom. We held each other tightly, bawling, as tears streamed down our faces.

Out of nowhere, Katrina appeared right next to me, her gun leveled at the man. Positioned nearby, the other women stood armed and prepared, ready to launch an attack against him.

"Toss me the keys to the van. Then you have ten seconds to explain who you are and why you have Megan's mother before I shoot you and leave you for animal bait," ordered Katrina.

"No, wait! He's with me, Megan. He's been helping me find you. This is Antonio Perez, from the ship," said my mom, placing a hand over his arm. "He's the security captain."

"Why are you in the kidnapper's van?" I asked.

"It's a long story. We saw them taking you off the ship unconscious. We chased them and lost them, but then saw the van again on the highway. We got the driver to pull over, then he pulled a gun on our taxi driver and took off. But the captain here was smart enough to check the GPS on the van, and we've been watching the house where you were being held. Of course, we weren't sure you were there. Not until we saw you all leave."

"Wow. So how did you figure all this out, Mom? That's impressive. But before we say anything else, I have to tell you something about the people who took us," I stressed, dreading telling my mother that Rochelle was behind my abduction.

"I already know. It was Rochelle. I overheard her and Nate talking, and that's when we put everything together."

"Where are the police? Why aren't they here? Have you called them?" asked Katrina.

"We can't. Rochelle and Nate paid off someone in the police department and the medical examiner's office to say Megan's body was recovered at the bottom of a ravine, the victim of a car accident. We called the FBI, but because they think they have a positive ID for Megan, they won't help. Obviously, they will now when she turns up alive."

"Rochelle told me all that. I guess she couldn't resist bragging about how brilliant her plan was. My God. They have this all figured out, don't they?" I gasped.

"Would it be possible for you ladies to lower your weapons, miss? Before someone gets shot accidentally?" asked Captain Perez, glancing at Katrina nervously.

"I can handle a firearm. If I shoot you it won't be an accident," said Katrina, lowering her arm to relax by her side, while the other women followed suit. "So, what do we do now, then?" she asked.

"Yeah. If the FBI won't help and we can't go to the police, then what are our options?" I asked.

"I have an idea. But first, let's get you all back to the ship safely and have the ship's doctor give you all a quick checkup to make sure no one needs medical attention," said Perez.

"We're fine. Nothing a hot shower and a decent meal won't fix," replied Katrina.

"All right. Let's get back to the ship. I'll call ahead and have my staff prepare a couple of rooms. We aren't completely sold out for this trip, so I can put you up in a couple of suites. It might be a little crowded, but it will only be for one night. We will be back in Los Angeles tomorrow evening," said Perez.

"We've just spent the past week on filthy mattresses shackled to the wall of a dark basement, eating cold beans and rice, and using buckets as toilets. Anything you give us will surpass that by a mile," said Katrina.

Perez lowered his head. "I'm so sorry you had to go through that. The people responsible for this will pay. I give you my word. I will do all I can to bring them to justice."

"That's all we can ask of you. Thank you. And thank you for helping my mom find us. I knew she would never stop looking for me," I said, hugging her tightly.

"I knew something was wrong. Rochelle kept trying to convince me you went looking for Brian. We even went to his hotel to see him," replied my mom, wiping her eyes.

"You did what? Oh my God, Mom. You know I would never do that," I cried.

"Well, I was out of options at that point. Security had searched the ship for you and said maybe you went overboard. I was desperate for answers, Megan. But I now know that Mateo, the security officer, was in on the scheme with Rochelle and Nate."

"Yes, we are all acquainted with Mateo," I sneered. I shuddered at the thought of his corpse lying in the basement of the house.

Katrina shot me a look, and I subtly shook my head. I wasn't prepared to unpack all of that right now. Honestly, I wasn't sure I ever would be. I knew eventually I would have to disclose to the police what happened to Mateo and what I did to the other guard on the ship. The man Rochelle killed following my attack on him. But at that moment, I was so emotionally overwhelmed, I just couldn't bring myself to say anything.

"We need to get out of here. The buyers are coming tonight to get us, and I don't want to be anywhere near here when they show up." I shuddered, chills running down my spine at the mere thought of crossing paths with them.

Following Perez, we all crammed into the van, where he unloaded and stored the guns under the seats. With just eight seats and twelve of us, a couple of the girls sat behind the seats in the cargo hold. Perez and my mom adjusted their seats to make space for two of the smallest women on the van floor. Despite the awkward seating, we were all relieved to be leaving. Perez called ship security once we were on the highway and arranged the preparation of the only two available rooms for the women.

"So how are we going to get this Rochelle woman and that asshole, Nate?" asked Katrina.

"They need to confess. I think the only play here is to have Rochelle come to my room and have Megan there. I can record her confession," suggested my mom.

"I need to be there. I cannot allow you to be bait, Michelle," Perez declared, glancing over at my mom.

"She won't talk if you're there, Antonio. But I know her well enough to know that she will sing like a canary to me once she knows she's been caught out. She will want to prove to me that she's still smarter than all of us," replied my mom.

Antonio? Michelle?

My mom and Captain Perez seemed to be on familiar terms. I wondered when that happened?

"Then I'll stay out of sight. I can hide in the bathroom or the closet. But I am not leaving you alone with that woman."

"That's fair. I'll call her when we get back on the ship," said my mom.

"I'd like to be a fly on the wall when she gets taken down," snickered Katrina.

I relaxed in my seat, thankful that this terrifying ordeal was coming to a close. However, my worries persisted. Was there really a chance that Rochelle would confess? Without a confession, was there enough evidence to link her to the abductions? It might come down to my word against hers. Among us, I was the sole person who interacted with or witnessed Rochelle's involvement. Our only choice was to ensure her confession. I was going to make that happen, no matter the cost.

CHAPTER THIRTY-EIGHT

Megan

The van raced down the highway, headed toward Playa del Carmen. I stayed focused on the view outside, thinking about all the challenges both I and the women with me had faced. It was still so unbelievable that Rochelle was the one behind it all. I couldn't stop replaying in my head all the things I wanted to say to her. I had so many unanswered questions. As the fear and shock subsided, anger took its place. And for the first time in my life, I allowed myself to embrace my rage with no guilt. I had every reason to be pissed off, and I wouldn't suppress it this time like I usually did. I was putting an end to me going along to get along.

My mom let out a small cry and withdrew her hand from mine. I was unaware that I was squeezing her hand so tightly, preoccupied with thoughts of Rochelle.

"Sorry, Mom," I apologized, rubbing the top of her hand.

"It's okay, sweetie. Just try to stay calm. I know this has been a terrible experience. But it's over now," she replied.

"It's far from over, Mom. But I'll try to keep my feelings in check," I said, giving her a small smile.

Truthfully, the closer we got to Playa del Carmen and the *Jewel of the Sea*, the more nervous I became. When we reached the dock and I caught sight of the ship, a shiver raced down my spine and I started to have second thoughts about our decision to confront Rochelle. I wished Captain Perez would just detain her and Nate and let the FBI deal with them. But I knew without her confession, there was a chance she could escape justice with the right attorney. She was undeniably smart enough and organized enough not to leave a trail of evidence that could lead back to her. Given everything she had made me and the other women endure, you'd think this would be the easy part for me. But it wasn't. I was overwhelmed with both fear and apprehension. So much was riding on the outcome of this. Still, I felt a duty to all the women Rochelle had abducted before me, who were now lost forever.

Perez parked the van in close proximity to the ship and called two officers to escort us on board. Another officer was monitoring Rochelle, who was relaxing at the pool, completely oblivious that her criminal enterprise was about to implode. Nate was also under surveillance at a casino. As we were ushered onto the ship, we attracted quite a few curious stares from fellow passengers. At the infirmary, we were checked for dehydration and general wellness. Once we were given clearance by the medical staff, Perez had officers escort us to our rooms, where he assured us we would be safe. I predicted most of the women would opt for a hot meal and a shower before heading straight to bed. I wouldn't be so lucky, as I still faced the difficult task of getting Rochelle to confess.

Being back in the stateroom brought me a tremendous sense of relief. I asked my mom and Perez to give me time to take a hot shower and change into my own clothes before we called Rochelle. I let the hot water cascade over me, hoping it would help me calm down. Although I was still anxious about confronting Rochelle, I also felt a sense of pride in myself. I had navigated through a traumatic experience without crumbling, and I achieved things in the last five days that I never imagined possible. I felt more self-assured after that thought, and by the time I finished showering, I was as mentally prepared as I could be to face Rochelle.

When I came out of the bathroom, my mom and Perez were sitting on the couch together. I missed what my mom said to him, but he responded by laughing and tilting his head back. It made me happy to see my mom enjoying herself with a man, a sight I hadn't seen since my dad's passing.

Perez faced me and smiled. "I've called the FBI agent handling your case and briefed him on the latest developments. We've agreed that I'll keep Rochelle and Nate detained onboard in the ship's brig until we dock in Los Angeles tomorrow evening, where he'll meet us. At that point, Rochelle and Nate will be taken into custody, and you and the other women will be interviewed. By that time, we should have Rochelle's confession forwarded to the FBI."

"Are the other women going to be able to contact their families? They've been missing for two weeks now," I asked.

"The agents are currently talking to each of them and collecting their families' contact details. They will notify their families to let them know that the women have been recovered and are on their way home," he replied.

"One of the women died while captive. Her name was Desiree," I said.

"Yes. Katrina told me about her and the FBI is aware."

"Okay, so how is this going to work?" I asked.

"I will be in the bathroom with one of my officers. Your mom will hide her cell phone in her pocket, and it will record everything said. My officer should arrive any moment, and he will hide a listening device in the room as well. Once he is here, your mom will try to reach Rochelle. She left the pool about thirty minutes ago and went back to her cabin."

I sipped a cup of coffee and attempted to relax, but I couldn't sit still. Once the security officer and Perez took their places, hiding in the bathroom, I joined my mom on the bed and listened while she called Rochelle's room. As the phone rang, I became anxious that Rochelle wouldn't pick up. When she finally did, my heart started to race.

"Rochelle? It's me. I know. I'm sorry I worried you. I just needed some alone time to think. But I'm much better now. I have news. Can you come to my room right away? I'd rather wait to tell you until you get here. Okay, see you shortly."

With a trembling hand, my mom placed the receiver back on the hook. Her performance was worthy of an Oscar. Rochelle wouldn't have any reason to be suspicious, as my mother sounded like she was near a breakdown. She reached over to squeeze my hand, and I reciprocated with a hug. It felt like hours before there was a knock on the door, when in reality it had only been five minutes. I stayed hidden behind the wall leading into the bedroom while my mom walked to the door to let Rochelle in.

"Michelle! Are you okay? What's the big news?"

"Come in, Rochelle. I have something to show you."

They rounded the corner, and Rochelle came to a sudden stop, her mouth falling open in disbelief at the sight of me. I was seated in the plush chair, my arms draped casually over the back, appearing far more relaxed than I actually was. Rochelle's mouth moved silently, opening and closing multiple times without uttering a word. I could see the shock register on her face, but she quickly concealed it.

"Megan! You're alive! Oh my God, we were so scared," she gasped, turning her back to my mom and taking two steps toward me, her arms open wide.

She gave me a piercing look, her lips pressed together in a tight line. It was obvious from her expression that she was furious. I wasn't surprised. My unexpected return to the ship, alive and well, was a major obstacle in her plan. I grinned at her and sat up straighter.

"Enough, Rochelle. Your secret is out so you can drop the act now. My mom knows everything. And don't come any closer to me, you psycho bitch."

CHAPTER THIRTY-NINE

Megan

"What are you talking about, Megan?" asked Rochelle, speaking to me, but twisting to look at my mom.

"How could you, Rochelle?" asked my mom, tears welling in her eyes.

I watched Rochelle physically shrink in front of me. Glancing between me and my mom, she recovered hastily and sat on the couch, crossing her legs.

"Well. It seems you are both up to speed, doesn't it? I didn't want to Michelle. You both must realize that. However, I was in an impossible situation and I needed to fix it. It was nothing personal. I don't know how you got away from Mateo, but I'm afraid I must insist that he take you to the holding house as planned, Megan. I need ten girls for delivery, and that's the bottom line. Please don't make Nate hurt your mother."

"We've already called the FBI, Rochelle. Megan isn't going anywhere. All the women have been safely rescued," said my mom.

Rochelle laughed. "That's clearly not the case or I would be in the brig right now with one of those inept glorified security guards who play police. There are people who work for me all over this ship, Michelle. One call and both of you will disappear forever. I don't want to hurt you, but Megan is going back. You can say goodbye to her first. And at least this way you'll have some closure."

Rochelle was obviously batshit crazy, and I was angry at myself all over again for not seeing it before. I resisted the urge to flatten her where she stood.

"You are insane, Rochelle, if you think my daughter is leaving this ship with Nate or Mateo or anyone else associated with you. And it was nothing personal? How dare you say that to me? This is as personal as it gets! You are a sociopath."

"Oh, Michelle. Don't be so naïve. Your entire world is always sunshine and lollipops. It gets so tiresome. Do you have any idea how much detail goes into running an enterprise like this? No. Of course you don't. Well, let me tell you, trafficking is a tiring business. I never expected to be working this hard at my age, but well, what can I say? The money is just too good. I planned to retire to a tropical island in a few years, but I suppose I'll have to escalate that plan now, thanks to the two of you. What is it the Marines say? Adapt and overcome? Yes. Words to live by in my business."

She paused briefly and smiled. "Michelle, we both know this will be your word against mine. You're a mother so overcome with grief that you would accuse your best friend of such a horrible act. There is nothing to link me to any of this. Even you didn't suspect a thing after all these years. I will get away with it, just as I always have. I'm offering you a gift here, Michelle, because of our long friendship. Most families never get to say goodbye to their daughters when they are sold. Say farewell to Megan, Michelle. Don't screw up your only opportunity. Because I won't make the offer again."

While Rochelle continued to enjoy the sound of her own voice, droning on about how smart she was, and congratulating herself on a job well done, I blocked her out. I masked my fear in order to hide just how scared I truly was. It was obvious that Rochelle was capable of doing whatever was necessary to save herself, without a second thought for me or my mom. I forced myself to breathe in and out steadily, slowing my heartbeat. Once Rochelle finally finished her rant, I exchanged a look with my mom, confirming we had heard enough of her confession.

My mom stood up and walked to stand directly in front of Rochelle, locking her gaze on her.

"Antonio? I think we're finished here," yelled my mom.

There was confusion in Rochelle's eyes as she turned her gaze from my mom to me.

"What's wrong, Rochelle? Are you finally at a loss for words? I believe the phrase you're looking for is *oh shit*. It's over," I said, deliberately taunting her.

Coming out of the bathroom, Perez and his officer had their handcuffs at the ready. Rochelle jumped up from the couch and spun around to stare at them in shock. Did she seriously believe we hadn't reached out to the police? She obviously had an inflated opinion of her ability to control everything in her orbit. Rochelle made a sudden move toward my mom, but Perez intervened just in time while my mom quickly jumped out of reach. Rochelle put up a fight, but they eventually got the handcuffs on her.

"Did you get Nate?" I asked Perez.

"Yes, he is being detained in a cell pending arrest by the FBI tomorrow evening."

"I won't spend a day in jail. You've got nothing but my word against hers," bragged Rochelle, twisting to glare at me.

Pulling her cell phone from out of her sweater pocket, my mom turned the screen toward Rochelle. "I have everything recorded, Rochelle. Your entire confession."

Rochelle screamed and fought to get loose from Perez's hold, but his grip remained firm.

"You bitch!" she shouted at my mom.

"Right back at you," I quipped.

Perez ordered his officer to transport Rochelle to the ship's brig, where I was certain she would spend a very uncomfortable night. It wouldn't be nearly as unbearable as our time as her captives, but it was a start. I was certain that a prison sentence wouldn't do Rochelle any favors once she was incarcerated there full time. Someone like her probably wouldn't survive long in that environment. Or she might surprise me and end up running the entire prisoner population. I didn't care either way. As long as she was locked up and couldn't do this to another woman ever again, that was good enough for me.

CHAPTER FORTY

Megan

The security officer led Rochelle from our cabin on her way to her holding cell. Her departure brought me relief, and the thought of the nightmare coming to an end made me even happier. Captain Perez went over what I should expect during my upcoming debriefing by the FBI, which put my mind further at ease.

He was about to leave when his phone rang. "Excuse me just a moment."

"Perez. What? Where is he now? Stay there. Call the infirmary and get a medic over there. Get a few officers to the exits immediately! She cannot get off this ship."

"What happened?" I asked, panic already coursing through me.

"Rochelle got away. A crew member knocked out my officer, and they took his handcuff keys and radio. Stay here and lock the door. Do not open your door to anyone but me. Do you understand? No one but me. Not even security," he stressed as he hurried to the door.

I was rendered speechless. After Perez left, my mom made sure the door was locked, and we stood there in disbelief, looking at each other. How could this have happened? If she fled into Mexico, she would vanish indefinitely. Any sense of security I had would be gone forever. We would live in constant fear, always looking over our shoulders, uncertain if she would send someone to seek revenge against us. Shaking uncontrollably, I collapsed on the couch. This was the absolute worst thing that could have occurred. I glanced over at my mom and saw tears forming in her eyes.

"He'll get her, Mom. He has to," I shuddered.

She nodded in response and curled up on the bed. She seemed absolutely shattered, and it tore me apart to see her in that condition. The stress of Rochelle's betrayal, days of worrying about me, and now Rochelle's escape, had worn her out. I couldn't recall a single time when my mom had ever appeared her age until now. Sitting on the edge of the bed, I reached out to hold her hand. It was all I could do to comfort her.

The agony of waiting was unbearable. We were completely in the dark about what was unfolding, and my imagination ran wild with worst-case scenarios. I had a feeling my mom was likely doing the same thing. I felt like I was about to explode after waiting for two hours when a knock at the door made me jump. I hurried to the door and looked through the peephole. It was Perez.

"It's him!" I said, and my mom rushed to my side.

The moment I opened the door, I knew it wasn't good news. The captain's expression told me all I needed to know. He stepped inside and closed and locked the door behind him.

"We haven't been able to locate Rochelle. Nate is still obviously in custody, but is refusing to talk."

"Did she get off the ship?" asked my mom.

"We don't know for sure. I am inclined to think she did, yes. Her sea card was flagged as unauthorized to leave the ship, but she might have slipped through, especially if she had help from a crew member. We aren't certain how many ship employees are on her payroll. I've informed the FBI, and her passport has been frozen."

"Mexico is a big country, Captain. She could hide out here for a long time, undetected. What happened, exactly? How did she get away?" I asked.

"My officer was escorting her to the brig when another crew member approached them. He knocked my officer unconscious.

The officer didn't recognize the staff member. We have over one thousand employees on board, so it is impossible for him to know every one of them. He is reviewing employee ID cards to see if he can pick out his assailant. In the interim, please stay in your room and keep the door locked for your safety."

"You don't have to worry about that, Captain. The last thing we want is a confrontation with anyone associated with Rochelle's operation."

CHAPTER FORTY-ONE

Megan

The rest of the evening was filled with restless attempts to keep ourselves busy while stuck in the cabin. Even if we had been allowed to, I didn't have the energy to make it to the dining room. Perez had us request room service and escorted the waiter to deliver it to our room. I felt like I was in the Witness Protection Program. The other women were getting the same treatment, and I had no doubt they were just as unhappy about the situation after being trapped in a basement for a week. Despite the stress, I easily fell into a deep sleep right after dinner and didn't wake up until the alarm went off at six o'clock the following morning.

Perez called just after 7:00 a.m. to confirm that Rochelle had definitely left the ship. The FBI located the cab driver she hailed at the docks. They also found the crew member who assisted her in escaping, and upon learning the charges he was facing, he wisely cooperated with them.

I knew this was going to be an emotional day for my mother. For me too. Our return to Los Angeles and our everyday lives were mere hours away. Although nothing would ever be normal for either of us after this, especially with Rochelle on the loose. I had kept my anxiety in check last night, but this morning, I could already feel the nerves beginning to resurface. It would be a huge challenge for someone like me to move on from this experience. I was already more irrationally anxious and fearful than most people, and I was worried about the impact this would have on my future. I pushed the thought out of my mind for the time being. I had to give my full attention to getting through this day and my impending interview with the FBI.

Later that afternoon, with no word about Rochelle yet, we packed and waited for Perez to come and escort us to the security office, where we would wait to disembark. He arrived a couple of hours before we were ready to dock in Los Angeles, and we walked into the office to see Katrina and the others were already there. The atmosphere was filled with anticipation and an undercurrent of anxiety as everyone looked forward to going home. I was having trouble remaining calm, and I couldn't shake my growing sense of unease. I had never been in contact with law enforcement in an official capacity, but now I faced an FBI interview. The thought was unsettling, to say the least. Next to me, Katrina reached out and clasped my hand. She inched closer to me and spoke in a hushed voice.

"If it weren't for you, none of us would be here, you know. If everything had gone as planned, we would have been handed off to our buyers last night and by this morning we could have been anywhere. Thank you, Megan."

I gave her hand a gentle squeeze. "You were pretty amazing yourself, Katrina. I was driven by sheer desperation and fear when I took Mateo down. I had no intention of killing him."

I felt a constant urge to tell that to anyone willing to listen. Killing Mateo wasn't something I was proud of. I regretted it, and wanted to make that clear.

"I was just trying to disable him. You, on the other hand, took charge and got us out of that place with no hesitation," I said.

She smiled at me and shrugged. "What can I say? I'm a control freak by nature."

We both laughed, and I felt some of the stress ease out of me.

"You've got this, girlfriend. Just tell your truth and then you can go home and put your life together again. You're so lucky. You've got your mom to help you," she said.

I glanced over at my mom, who was talking to Nicole. "Yes, I am lucky to have her," I remarked. "What about you, Katrina? Who do you have to help you through this?"

She grinned and glanced down. "Don't worry about me. I always get through."

I got the impression she was alone, and I wanted to ask her more, but she was already caught up in conversation with the woman next to her, and I missed my chance to ask.

We arrived at the port of Los Angeles a couple of hours later, and soon after that, Nate was escorted out of the brig by security. The officers walked him past us, but he never glanced in our direction. He no longer resembled the suave ladies' man he once was. His clothes were wrinkled, his hair was messy, and his eyes had dark circles under them. Silence filled the air as all of us watched him, even though he refused to even acknowledge our existence. It was a powerful moment. We had won, and he was well aware of it. I had to admit, seeing him in handcuffs filled me with a profound sense of satisfaction.

CHAPTER FORTY-TWO

Rochelle

I hopped into the taxi and twisted around to get a glimpse out the back window. There was no one chasing after me, and no one seemed to pay any attention to me. With a smile, I rotated and made myself at home in the backseat of the cab.

Idiots. Every last one of them. It was so simple to get away. It was a pity that Nate was apprehended, but since I was now being pushed into retirement earlier than expected, I no longer had any need for him anyway. It was quite surprising, though, that among all the girls I had trafficked over the years, Megan was the one who ultimately took down my operation. Timid, scared little Megan. Well, I guess you just never really know what someone is capable of until they are tested. It would be wise for her and her mother to remember that, because I had no intention of going to prison. Ever. Given my age, it would be a suicide trip. The idea of being confined to a tiny cell for twenty-three hours a day, either alone or, worse yet, with a criminal stranger as a roommate, made me shudder.

Returning to my beautiful home would be impossible for me now. However, I had previously arranged with my attorney for exactly this kind of situation. In my business, one can never be too safe or too prepared. I left my home and a nice nest egg for my cousin, Natalie, in New Hampshire. While we didn't stay in touch regularly, the memories of growing up with her remained dear to me. I hoped this would be a nice surprise for her. With the money in my offshore accounts, I could live in luxury for two lifetimes. Under an assumed name, of course. As I mentioned before, one must always exercise caution in my line of work.

I guided the taxi driver down a quiet street and signaled for him to stop in front of an alley. I paid him in pesos and proceeded to an unremarkable, very forgettable door set into the brick of the building. I knocked on the door three times, waited, and then tapped it twice more. Through a small iron grate at the top of the door, a barrier opened slightly, revealing a deep brown eye staring back at me. The eye widened in surprise when they saw me at their door.

"It's me, Ricardo. Let me in. I need your help. I need to leave the country immediately," I barked.

I heard the lock on the door turn and I was inside and out of the alley in under thirty seconds.

The man eyed me briefly before ushering me inside.

"I need a passport under the name of Lauren Medina. ASAP. I need to fly out this evening. How long will that take you?"

"Maybe two hours. Maybe more, maybe less. Who knows?" he replied, his heavy accent making it a little difficult to understand him.

"Fine. I'll wait," I agreed, tossing my purse on the couch and taking a seat.

He made no move to leave, standing there staring at me.

"*Rápido.* The clock is ticking," I pointed out, tapping the face of my watch.

He walked off to the back room, while I made myself comfortable on the couch and booked a flight from Cancun to Seychelles International Airport. I had no other option but to embark on a day and a half journey, including an overnight layover, to reach my destination. I drifted off and woke up ninety minutes later to Ricardo shaking me awake. He was standing in front of the couch, staring at me again. He was a peculiar little man. Yet, he was the most talented forger in this specific part of Mexico. Because I had employed his services in the past, he already had my picture and information on record. I gazed at the picture staring back at me from the passport. It may have been a few years old, but it was still usable. I reached into my purse and passed him the fee for the passport. With a quick call, a taxi arrived, and I was soon on my way to the airport.

The process of getting through security and onto my flight seemed never-ending. Once I was settled into my seat, I finally felt a sense of relief. I had done it. I was on my way to freedom. I couldn't help smiling to myself as I gazed out the window at the setting sun and the runway below. But my serenity was short-lived when flashing lights caught my attention, and I immediately sat up straighter. I watched as three black SUVs and two local police units raced across the tarmac, making a beeline for my plane. I tried to convince myself that it could be absolutely anything. They weren't necessarily coming for me. Even so, my heart quickened as the doors of the vehicles were flung open. A group of men, along with two women, hurried toward the aircraft. Their jackets billowed in the wind, revealing gun holsters and badges fastened to their belts. As the agents boarded, my focus shifted to the front of the plane. They made their way down the aisle, taking note of every person. As soon as they got to my seat, I realized it was the end.

An agent bent down, gripping my arm, and forcefully removing me from my seat.

"Rochelle Kendrick, you are under arrest for trafficking by force and kidnapping."

I remained completely silent. I knew better than to open my mouth. I would rely on my attorney to get me out of this mess. I paid him a ridiculously large sum of money as a monthly retainer to be at my disposal. I was on the verge of finding out if he was worth his exorbitant fees.

CHAPTER FORTY-THREE

Megan
TWO MONTHS LATER

My therapy was going well. I wouldn't say I was against mental health treatment before I went on the cruise. I just wasn't aware of its potential benefits. Through counseling, I addressed the trauma of captivity, my guilt over Mateo's death, the guard's death on the ship, and the betrayal by Nate and Rochelle. I was even working on processing my emotions from the breakup with Brian. As expected, canceling my wedding proved to be a difficult task. My doctor had a lot to unpack with me. Above all, my treatment enabled me to become braver in my day-to-day life, taking small steps at a time. I was challenging myself to do more things outside of my comfort zone. Don't get me wrong—I had no intention of running out to buy self-help books or watching the Dr. Phil show, but I couldn't deny that it was making a difference.

Yes, something bad happened to me on the cruise. What Rochelle and Nate almost got away with doing to us was unthinkable. But I pulled through and came out of the other side a stronger person. I've always known that life could throw some curveballs, but what I'd recently realized was what truly mattered was our response and how we let those curveballs shape us. Despite our best efforts to exert control, life would always unfold on its own terms. Life was always going to do its thing in the end. Being forcibly abducted, imprisoned, and nearly sold into sex slavery was an incredibly challenging ordeal. And it was definitely not something I'd ever want to repeat. I always chuckled when I recalled my mom's words as she tried to convince me to join her and Rochelle on the cruise. She had dubbed it a cruise to forget. It turned out she was right. It absolutely was a cruise to forget—but for all the wrong reasons. However, I held onto the hope that one day I could forget it.

Although I was trying hard to put my abduction behind me, I'd stayed in touch with Katrina. I liked her, but we would never be friends who would hang out together on a regular basis. She was too wild for me, even post-therapy. She was currently on a solo backpacking tour somewhere in Germany. We had both sworn off cruises, but I was still getting out more. I even had a camping trip to Yosemite planned with some friends from work in a couple of weeks. Surprisingly, I was actually looking forward to it. Although I still didn't trust myself to go online and research Yosemite. I knew a lot of people went missing there on camping trips each year, and I couldn't let myself fall into that paranoid trap. So I relied on some coping skills my therapist taught me and had resisted the temptation so far. That was a huge accomplishment for me.

Rochelle's capture and extradition back to the United States brought me a sense of safety, as both she and Nate were behind bars. But I still had reservations about giving testimony against them in court. Although I knew they couldn't harm me anymore, I wasn't excited about revisiting all the painful memories and reliving the experience. Feeling conflicted between what was convenient and what was morally correct was not easy. But Katrina and the other women would be there to testify with me, and that was helpful.

No charges were filed against me in Mateo's death or the assault on the guard I attacked on the ship, as it was determined I acted in self-defense in both instances. However, I still carried a heavy burden of guilt over their deaths, despite everything. When the FBI raided the trap house, Mateo's body and the two other guards were no longer there. The assumption was made that the buyers had found them and taken care of their mess. They had completely cleared out the house, as if nobody had ever set foot inside. Rochelle's financial records were still under the scrutiny of the FBI, leaving open the possibility of catching the buyers at a later date. I hoped that some of the women Rochelle had sold could be located and rescued.

It was difficult to move on because our rescue and the takedown of the trafficking operation remained front page news for much longer than I had hoped it would. It was the happy ending that kept the story going. That, and people loved the drama. The upside was that it drew attention and put the human trafficking issue in the spotlight, which could potentially have a positive impact. I genuinely hoped so. There wasn't a day that passed when I didn't think about all the women before me who had been tragically sold into sex slavery. Those women were daughters, sisters, girlfriends, even wives and mothers. My heart ached for them and their loved ones. I organized a 4k run to raise awareness, hoping that my contribution might encourage others to adopt the "see something, say something" mentality.

Because of what I went through, my life had been completely altered. There were some good and some bad aspects. But I was confident I would get through it. Brian and I hadn't spoken or crossed paths since the day he left our house. However, a few weeks ago at the mall, Tracy bumped into him with Leticia. According to her, Brian appeared worn out and done in. I couldn't tell if she said that to console me after the breakup or if he was genuinely unhappy.

The truth was, Brian being miserable wasn't necessary for my own happiness. I was in the process of moving on. Of course, I was still hurt over his decision to leave me for that aspiring Tammy Faye Baker look-alike and probably would be for a while. Obviously, overcoming my resentment toward both Brian and Leticia was still a work in progress for me.

The good news was that a new teacher started working at school, and there was some innocent flirting happening between us. Having learned my lesson, I was taking things slowly, but I was also fairly certain the new teacher wouldn't drug and abduct me like Nate had. Maybe with a little luck, things would heat up on our teachers' trip to Yosemite. I knew, given the chance, Tracy would make sure she did everything in her power to make that happen. She was my biggest cheerleader when it came to my love life.

I had been prioritizing spending more time with my mom recently too. Her single-minded determination in rescuing me made me see her in a whole new light, and I had a new appreciation for her. She had really showed up for me. Had it not been for her, my disappearance might have otherwise remained unsolved forever. In addition, she had to come to terms with the shocking revelation that her bestie of twenty years, Rochelle, wasn't the person she thought she was. I made sure she got out to the senior center a couple of days each week, where she was forming new friendships. She had even gone on a couple of day trips to local casinos with her new pals, and that seemed to help her in dealing with the loss of Rochelle's friendship. Antonio and my mom were also spending some quality time together since he had retired from the cruise ship security business. I liked him. He appeared to be a nice guy, and it made me happy that my mom had someone to spend time with.

So overall, things were good. Or at the very least, getting better with each passing day. What had I learned from all of this? If there was one thing I took away, it was that in the end, family and friends were all that truly mattered. Everything else was just insignificant background noise. Meaningless distractions. Unimportant minutiae. Treasure your loved ones and don't sweat life's small stuff.

And don't forget, life is going to do its thing, and it is unpredictable. So embrace it with open arms. Because you never know what surprise awaits you around the next corner.

THE END

ABOUT THE AUTHOR

Christy Cooper-Burnett is an award-winning author based in southern California with a degree in Administration of Justice. She has one grown son who inspired her to write her award-winning debut novel, *No Way Home.*

She enjoys creating relatable stories and characters that encourage readers to imagine what they would do if thrown into the same unique situations as her strong female protagonists. Christy's novels have received numerous awards.

Christy comes from a long line of police officers and worked in crime prevention early in her career. When she's not writing, she's been known to binge watch series in a single weekend, throw dinner parties, and will travel anywhere at a moment's notice as long as her rescue beagle Gertie can tag along.

OTHER TITLES BY
CHRISTY COOPER-BURNETT

NOTE FROM
CHRISTY COOPER-BURNETT

Word-of-mouth is crucial for any author to succeed. If you enjoyed *Missing*, please leave a review online—anywhere you are able. Even if it's just a sentence or two. It would make all the difference and would be very much appreciated.

Thanks!
Christy Cooper-Burnett

We hope you enjoyed reading this title from:

www.blackrosewriting.com

Subscribe to our mailing list – *The Rosevine* – and receive **FREE** books, daily
deals, and stay current with news about upcoming
releases and our hottest authors.
Scan the QR code below to sign up.

Already a subscriber? Please accept a sincere thank you for being a fan of
Black Rose Writing authors.

View other Black Rose Writing titles at
www.blackrosewriting.com/books and use promo code
PRINT to receive a **20% discount** when purchasing.